Uly Quits His Job

TRAVIS WILLIAMS

For my mother, Linda Williams

Contents

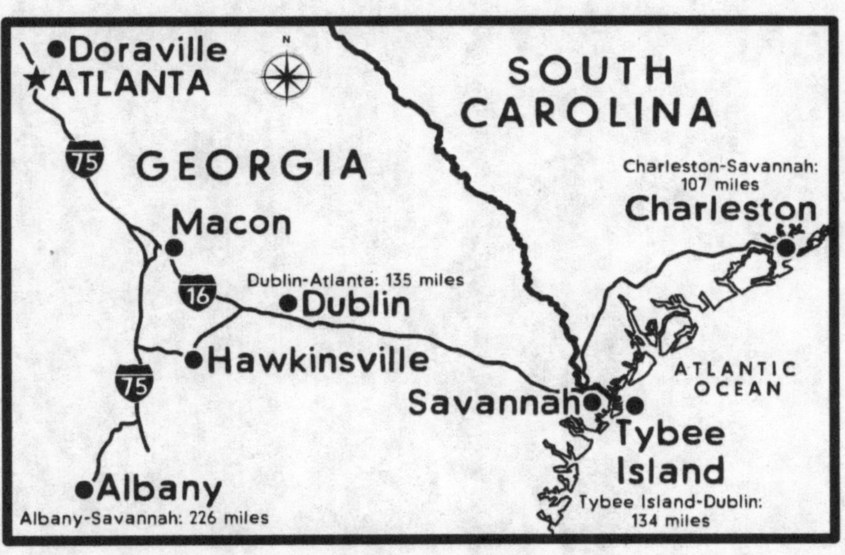

Doraville
ATLANTA
N
SOUTH CAROLINA
GEORGIA
75
Charleston-Savannah:
107 miles
Charleston
Macon
Dublin-Atlanta: 135 miles
16
Dublin
Hawkinsville
ATLANTIC OCEAN
75
Savannah
Tybee Island
Albany
Tybee Island-Dublin:
134 miles
Albany-Savannah: 226 miles

PROLOGUE
Newton Dewberry's Go-Kart

Ten-year-old Uly scrunched up his face and looked at the inert hunk of rusty iron sitting on the table.

It was a five-horsepower Briggs & Stratton gasoline engine. The oil had been replaced with rust.

Uly's friend, Newton Dewberry, stood next to him, feet fidgeting, watching and waiting while Uly took his time looking at the ancient thing.

Newton's older brothers had installed it on the go-kart many years ago. Then they deliberately rode it to destruction, doing nothing to take care of it.

Newton whined, "Yoo-lee," emphasizing his frustration by kicking a leg of the cobbled-together table standing on the thick, dry, dusty timbers of the floor of his family's old barn. "I know you can fix any go-kart engine! I seen you do it."

Newton didn't know about helping verbs.

Uly protested right back, louder than necessary. "Newton Dewberry!" He liked saying Newton's full name. "Nobody never put no oil in that engine never!"

Uly knew the rule about double negatives, but he liked piling them on anyway.

Newton pouted. "Well, it prob'ly had some once." Then he mumbled something about it not being his fault.

Uly reached for the little engine and rocked it on the table. "And it ain't been sitting on this table long. I know, 'cause it used to be sitting on that go-kart." Uly turned and pointed. "Out there."

The sun was shining brightly in the dirt yard outside the barn's gaping maw of an entrance.

Uly looked at Newton and continued. "In the rain. Every day for a million years! It's seized up! It's a single chunk of iron. I can fix any go-kart engine, including this one, but I cain't fix it today. And today is when we are."

He made "can't" rhyme with "ain't."

Newton looked at his friend and nodded. "So, we improvise."

A grin spread across Uly's face. "We don't need no engine, Newton Dewberry—we need speed!"

Newton smiled big, "You got a good idea, doncha, Uly?"

"Help me push the go-kart out to the driveway."

Newton always did what Uly said because Uly always had good ideas.

However, Newton had learned the hard way that his faith in Uly was not shared by everyone. He remembered the day his mom had slammed the door behind her as they walked into their house. She turned and glared at her son after one of Uly's good ideas had not turned out exactly the way the boys had anticipated. "Newton! Uly never has a good idea, son. They. Are. All. Bad!"

He pursed his lips and mumbled, "It seemed okay at the time. It wasn't my fault that—"

"You need to use good judgement! Next time ask yourself whether the end of one of Uly's ideas is anything you want to be standing around for. In fact, you know what? There's not going to be a next time because—"

"But no one knows the future. Sometimes—"

"Newton! Y'all were playing with gasoline! You can predict what happens when you put a match to gasoline."

"It wasn't a match, it was ... "

The conversation didn't go well after that, but that was almost a year ago.

Uly and Newton had stayed out of trouble for the most part in recent months. Also, this go-kart was as harmless as a go-kart could get.

It wasn't remotely new. In fact, it had belonged to Newton's father when he was a boy. The go-kart was made from a rectangular sheet-metal platform on a frame of iron tubes. These were welded together at the four corners with two more braces stretched from one side to the other. Four wheels were attached to simple mounts.

All the parts were welded together. Apparently, the go-kart factory hadn't believed in nuts and bolts.

An upside-down V of metal tubes was positioned off-center to the left and held the steering wheel in place. At the front, the wheels were connected to steering arms which were connected to a joint on the steering column. Behind that were two little levers on brackets. One was the gas pedal and the other was the brake pedal. Both had been decommissioned.

They were definitely not playing with gasoline this time.

Behind the steering wheel, a tubular frame, also welded together, originally held two pieces of lumber. One served as a seat for two children to ride side by side and the other, if it hadn't been missing, would have served as a seat back. The seat was partially covered in torn, cheap red vinyl. The rusted sheet-metal platform behind the seat was empty since the most recent engine was on the table in the barn.

Half the welded joints were broken because the go-kart had at some point become a project in the hands of the notorious Dewberry twins, Newton's older brothers. They had expressed some displeasure with the design because, in their words, "It was built for babies."

It originally came with a two-horsepower Honda engine with the governor cranked down to decrease the available horsepower. This was a prudent design for a toy go-kart for small children.

Newton's brothers—now grown and moved away—quickly grew tired of a baby go-kart when they were eight or nine years old because they no longer considered themselves babies. They modified the go-kart with a five-horsepower

Briggs & Stratton and then removed the spring from the governor. This little fix vastly increased the available horsepower. They also removed the muffler and the air filter to make the flow of air into and out of the engine as unobstructed as possible, further increasing the power of the engine, if not its longevity.

They then took turns driving their thoroughly hot-rodded little go-kart. While one drove, the other rode as a passenger holding on for dear life. They would take turns driving at highway speeds around the barn. Not just driving but spinning doughnuts to the left in an effort to launch the other brother as far as possible into the dusty yard.

This effort never failed to produce the desired result, which was for the brother riding shotgun to go skittering and bouncing across the ground, spinning like a log rolling uncontrolled down a hillside.

The farthest distance one could launch a passenger was never recorded, but it was considerable.

Neither brother ever admitted to being hurt by any of this foolishness. By the time they grew tired of this game and were getting too big to sit behind the steering wheel, their antics had all but destroyed the go-kart, which was built for babies, not big, rambunctious boys who had been taught how to wrench on an engine.

Uly walked beside the left side and steered the go-kart as they pushed it out toward the dirt drive past the barnyard area. "The steering wheel works, Newton Dewberry."

Glancing up from the back, Newton warned Uly. "But it ain't got no brakes."

Uly stopped and looked down the long slope of dry, compact Georgia red clay that served as the driveway up to the barn.

A quiet, paved country road crossed the end of the driveway at the bottom of the hill. When was the last time a car went by on this road?

Not only was this a road that connected nothing to nothing, there was a creek on the other side of the road opposite the end of the driveway.

A dense growth of tall shrubbery hid a bend in the creek, which at that point was wider, relatively speaking, than it was in other areas. It was deep next to the road where it eroded the bank and shallow on the other side where it had deposited a sandbar.

Occasionally, Newton and Uly had jumped into the swimming hole from the side of the road. The area was too snaky for Uly's liking, so he usually recommended other ways of having fun without admitting to Newton he was afraid of snakes.

Finally, he spun around and spoke to Newton, "We don't need brakes."

He took one more look at the slope of the driveway and the distance to the road while making some mental calculations. "Now, here's the plan, Newt. We get in the go-kart and sit down and then 'Fred Flintstone' it backwards down the driveway to get some speed. Then right before we get to the road, I'll turn the steering wheel hard to spin us around the other way, so we stop and don't zoom out into the road."

Newton nodded. "Okay."

Uly sat on the seat and twisted around so he could see behind them. Then he and Newton kicked to make the go-kart roll backwards down the slope of the driveway.

They kept kicking, picking up more speed, and rattled backwards down the dirt path with Uly driving.

When they were almost to the end of the driveway, they both realized they should stop kicking. Uly spun the steering wheel hard, and the go-kart whipped around in a one-hundred-and-eighty-degree turn that almost dislodged Newton from the passenger seat. A last loud creak and clang made them wonder if another weld broke somewhere.

The boys laughed.

Newton sat there. "That was pretty fun."

Uly looked both ways down the road. "Yeah. I guess."

"Uly, we need more speed."

Uly nodded, thinking. "There's hardly ever any cars on this road. If we don't stop right at the end of the driveway, it'll be okay, don't you think, Newton Dewberry?"

"Yeah."

"Let's push it back up and try again."

They pushed the go-kart the forty yards up the sloping drive to the barn.

Uly pointed. "You see that old bag of cement over next to

the barn? I know both of us can pick up a fifty-pound bag of feed each—"

"No way, Uly! I can't pick up a bag of feed. Why do we need that anyways?"

"It'll make us go faster."

"No, it won't."

Uly ignored him. "And that bag weighs eighty pounds, so if we work together, we can carry it over here to the go-kart and put it right here"—he pointed—"where the engine should be."

Newton grabbed a small limb that had fallen from a tree near the driveway. "We can chock the tires with this."

Uly agreed and jammed the stick behind the back tires. Then they went to get the bag of concrete.

It took more effort than they first imagined because the cement was a block in the shape of a bag. It had probably been sitting on the ground at the side of the barn since before Uly and Newton were born and had turned into a solid chunk. They were able to drag it over to the go-kart and then work it up onto the back. It filled the space perfectly behind the seat, but it squashed the dry-rotted old tires nearly flat.

Uly stood and looked at the flat tires with some exasperation. "Newton Dewberry—"

Newton was on his way into the barn already. "I'm on it."

He started a loud electric motor. A hissing, puffing sound came from the barn. Newton returned holding a tire inflator attached to a long red hose spiraling back into the barn. Uly was typically take-charge, but he let Newton inflate all the tires good and tight by himself.

Frowning, Uly shook his head. "There ain't no way the inner tubes are any good."

Uly lifted the back of the go-kart to take some of the weight of the concrete off the tires. Newton overinflated all four tires, almost like he wanted the inner tubes to pop, but for the moment, they all still held air. Then Newton tossed the inflator aside while the compressor inside the barn continued to chug.

Now that the tires were as full as ticks inflated to the point of almost bursting and the concrete weight was in place, Uly was certain this next ride down the driveway was going to be much more fun.

"I bet we do a full three-sixty at the bottom of the driveway this time," Newton said.

Uly adjusted the wheel-chocking limb. "Yeah. And we'll be going a lot faster! If we spin out into the road, we can push the go-kart out of the way before any cars come by."

Uly looked up at his friend. "Okay, Newton, when I say, 'push,' you push the limb to me from your side and then jump in. I'll pull the limb and throw it out of the way and jump in next to you at the same time. Got it?"

"Got it."

Uly put his hand on the limb and looked at Newton, who was already in position. The limb was pressed tight to the ground by the weight of the go-kart.

"Three, two, one, push!"

Newton pushed the limb hard, forcing it away from the

back wheel on his side. Uly yanked the limb and threw it aside, and both boys vaulted onto the seat with Uly behind the steering wheel.

The go-kart rolled back quickly.

Uly twisted around to see where they were going while Newton remained facing forward with a huge grin on his face.

Both boys only needed to push off once before they pulled their feet up onto the floor of the go-kart.

The mass of the concrete had stabilized the little vehicle and transferred most of the weight to the back tires. The extra weight didn't give them more speed. Instead, the overinflated tires remained perfectly round, which greatly reduced the amount of tread in contact with the ground and reduced friction to a fraction of what they had experienced on the first ride.

They traveled the forty yards between the barn and the road at almost half the speed of an object in free fall, which eventually would be an impressive forty-two miles per hour once they reached the end of the driveway.

The go-kart rattled and screeched, bouncing in great galloping hops as it careened down the driveway with its half-broken frame twisting out of shape with every bounce.

Uly was aware that Newton was screaming. It was the same scream Newton used when he jumped off a high limb in a tree with a rope tied around his waist. Which, for the record, had been a bad idea.

The first ride down the driveway hadn't been all that

thrilling. Now the end of the driveway approached at an alarming rate. They were practically already there!

And then something caught Uly's eye that wasn't there a second earlier. A sudden, cold knot of fear hit his stomach, and he started screaming with Newton.

An immense semitruck pulling a full-size trailer was barreling down the narrow country road at what looked like a hundred miles an hour.

Newton had no idea the semitruck was inbound and would be there in about three seconds. He was still screaming with a huge smile on his face as if he were on a roller coaster.

Uly heard the air horn on the truck and knew the driver had seen them—probably too late.

Six months earlier, Uly and Newton had announced to their parents that they were going to spend some time in the library. Being naturally curious, they were wanting to research their own names. This met with hearty approval from all the adults who knew them, and they were allowed to spend as much time as they wanted in the library if they were more or less well-behaved.

Newton discovered Newtonian mechanics and was quite proud of himself. Uly liked the subject as well and thought it was much more interesting, logical, and comprehensible than the source of his name: a long poem by a man named Homer who hadn't bothered to make it rhyme.

Their research into Isaac Newton inevitably led to information about Albert Einstein, who, they discovered, made the claim that matter and energy are made of the same thing and that time is relative as opposed to always being the same all the time everywhere.

Uly had been listening to Newton read aloud from a kids' book about the theory of relativity when he interrupted. "Newton Dewberry! These claims of ole Albert Einstein are highly unlikely!"

"Yep, you're right, Uly."

But Uly didn't want to be accused of being boneheaded if new facts came along to prove his initial misgivings unfounded.

They sped down the driveway toward the country road at forty-two miles per hour. It was a country road that a random semitruck driver had decided was a good one to drive down that day. Uly noticed that everything seemed to be moving in slow motion while his brain kept on thinking at normal speed. He began to reconsider the facts he had learned regarding the special theory of relativity.

He realized that not only is all mass made of energy, but energy of one kind is related to all the other kinds. In addition, he had the extraordinary insight that he could measure anything with nothing but his mind and senses. As a result, Uly intuitively measured the speed of the go-kart and the speed of the truck and calculated the exact moment of the impending convergence of the two.

He then considered his options. One possibility was to spin the steering wheel, but that might not actually stop them and would definitely fling both boys off the go-kart in unpredictable directions, landing them in the middle of the road at the precise moment the semitruck arrived at the end of the driveway. The definition of a bad idea.

A second option was to impose the will of his mind over matter and cause the go-kart to fly away, avoiding the collision with the truck. That didn't seem to be working, and he didn't have time to practice.

Finally, he seriously considered the amount of brake power he could apply by dragging his foot on the ground. Then he decided, with his newfound understanding of relativity, he would be unable to stop the go-kart in time.

During those moments of heightened awareness brought on by extreme impending danger, when time seemed to be moving at a crawl while his brain accelerated, Uly realized that far from being wishful thinking, option two, flight, was in fact in their future.

The sloping driveway flattened out and crossed a culvert that was installed in the ditch parallel to the road. The hard-packed soil over this piece of engineering had eroded and settled over the years, leaving a slope up to the roadbed, which was slightly higher than the end of the driveway. These differences were insignificant to anyone in a car or even a bicycle.

Uly could hear the low-pitched droning hum of Newton's joyful, boyish screaming, the perceived pitch of which had been made low by the sound waves traveling slower in Uly's relative time perception than they normally would be. He also later swore to Newton he could detect a slight shift in all colors toward the red end of the spectrum for the same reason, but Newton didn't quite believe it.

While still experiencing hyperawareness, Uly could see the slight concave dip in the end of the driveway that sloped up to match the slight convex curvature of the roadbed. This, he calculated, would serve as a ramp; which, when they hit it traveling at a high speed, would launch their lightweight vehicle into the air and across the road with at least one long second to spare before the truck arrived in the same spot.

One second later, he was exactly right about all of this. However, he had failed to notice one thing about their ride.

They crossed over the culvert, dipped down into the slight depression there, and crossed onto the roadbed which bounced the boys and the go-kart up.

As the boys dropped back down on the seat, it was still descending against what remained of the strength of the horizontal side rails of the go-kart frame and the bounciness of the inflated tires. At the bottom of the downward bounce, the frame of the go-kart was spring-loaded.

As they began a second bounce back up, the go-kart seat rebounded with them, heaving them into the air with a mighty pitch like a double bounce on a trampoline, with the difference being they were traveling horizontally at nearly forty miles an hour.

Newton Dewberry's feet rose in front of him as he double bounced off the seat while flying backwards and sailing above the shrubs at the side of the road. Then, in pure astonishment, he watched as the semitruck he didn't know about crossed in front of him.

Uly was looking backwards when they became airborne. He rotated in the air so that he was facing the ground and watched as the disintegrating go-kart flew through the shrubbery and peppered the surface of the water with parts and shrapnel. His body continued to rotate, bringing the sky into view.

He became aware that they had missed the truck. His brain slipped back from emergency mode into normal, real-time speed. The low note of the truck's air horn rose in pitch as the truck tore by.

The boys, along with the chunk of concrete, hit the surface of the creek at angles, shedding kinetic energy into the water and creating a shock wave that spewed water into the air and onto the other side.

The dense concrete buried itself in the creek bottom, but the more buoyant boys joined the wave and settled into a few inches of water on the sandy inside turn of the creek.

Uly lay on his back with his head half buried in water and sand, blinking up at the sky as water from their splashdown dripped off the tree canopy above him. Newton had continued to rotate in the air and ended up facedown in the creek next to him. He flopped over a few feet from Uly and moaned.

"Uly, was that a truck?"

"Yes."

"We are okay, right?"

"Yes."

"Did you forget to do a three-sixty?"

"No."

"Why?"

"I decided not to so we wouldn't get hit by the truck."

"Yeah, okay. That was a good idea."

They still hadn't moved.

Newton looked into the canopy of the trees. A few drops of water were still falling from leaves near the creek.

He pointed. "Uly, is that a tire?"

"Looks like it, Newton Dewberry. It's all that's left of your go-kart. Guess I'll fix that engine next week."

ULY
Friday Afternoon

Twenty-eight-year-old Uly clomped over the squeaky heart pine flooring of the old farmhouse serving as his employer's offices. It was quitting time on Friday, and he was heading home for the weekend.

His employer was a contractor who provided utility pole inspection, treatment, and maintenance for electric utility companies. Uly had moved from Atlanta in north Georgia to Albany in south Georgia for this job.

When he told his girlfriend, Rachel, that he wanted to take this job, he wasn't sure how she would react. He had hoped she would be happy for him.

"That's a big move, Uly ... "

"It's a great job! They've already interviewed me twice."

"Kind of a small company, isn't it?"

"Well, um ... I mean. I need a good job."

He had left it at that. He didn't hear from the company for a while, so he didn't think he would get the job. That's when he made the mistake of telling Rachel he was staying. And then they called, wanting him to start work immediately. So he did.

It was a challenge to work in gnat-infested south Georgia in the blazing sun among endless cotton and peanut fields or stands of pine trees.

Joe, one of the foremen, was sitting at a desk near the front door in what had once been a dining room.

"Hey Uly!" Joe called.

"Joe! Hey! I've been looking for you. I was hoping you might let me transfer to your crew so—"

"Done. Mr. West has already approved having you reassigned to me for the trip next week."

Uly nodded and stopped walking as he reached the desk. "Okay, that's cool."

"That is if you're available on Sunday afternoon?"

"You're driving to Savannah, right?"

"Yes. Mr. West wants us there first thing Monday morning. I'm going to drive over on Sunday after church."

"Okay, that works for me. You know, Joe, what do you think? I could advance to foreman in another six months or so, right?"

Joe froze his face and his eyes darted left and right before he locked his gaze back on Uly. "Well, you've certainly got the potential to get there, Uly." He stood and gave Uly a manly buddy slap on the shoulder—but it was a little too hard for someone who was sober.

Joe adopted an enthusiastic tone "This'll be a great trip,

Uly. This is a great group of men who laugh big and eat bigger. Right up your alley!"

"Cool. Thanks, Joe. Savannah's nice, next to the ocean, no gnats, and there are places to enjoy some shade under a live oak. It'll be like a working vacation, right? Okay, see you." He tried to leave.

Joe smiled big. "Of course. And there is travel pay, a per diem, and over-time for travel."

"Cool. I'm ready to go right now, Joe! Well I'll see y'all Sunday."

"Alright. Glad you're excited about it. I've overseen a number of these trips now, so don't worry about anything. You're going to be a perfect fit for the team!"

Joe liked being positive and encouraging. He had gone to a leadership conference where he learned all about being genuine and how to communicate effectively. The work he had done to learn about leadership and persuasion had gotten him to his current position.

Uly nodded while he talked, wishing he could leave. Joe was about to start talking about himself, but Uly didn't want to interrupt or walk away from his boss while he was still talking.

"There are a lot of moving parts on these trips, Uly. You might not be ready for a foreman's position just yet, but we'll get you trained up in the next couple of years. I can coach you."

"Um. Okay. A'ight. I'll be here, Sunday!"

"Great! Oh, and check your mailbox on the way out for the details."

Uly turned to leave. He stopped at an open wooden cabinet on the wall that served as the internal mail system. It had at least a dozen pigeonholes labeled with employee's names. He pulled a memo printed on bright yellow paper out of his box.

"Departing No Later Than 2:00 pm!" was printed in bold at the top of the paper. Uly glanced farther down the page. There were lots of different typefaces in various sizes. Under the headline, Joe had a list of painfully obvious items to pack and a bunch of other bullet points Uly didn't take the time to read.

He folded the memo down to a credit-card-sized rectangle and put it in the back pocket of his work pants next to his wallet where he wouldn't lose it.

Uly liked his job and the pay was decent, but he tended to live from paycheck to paycheck. This was true though housing in Albany was less than half what he had been paying in the Atlanta area.

On the way home he stopped to buy gas for his old Ford F-150. He loved his truck more than he worried about gas mileage. His commute was short, so it wasn't a hardship, especially since he had a good job.

To buy gas, he pulled his wallet out of his back pocket. The work memo fell on the ground, so he picked it up.

Can't lose that.

He tucked it back into the pocket. Since he had forty bucks

in cash, he decided not to buy more than thirty dollars' worth of gas so he would have ten dollars to take with him on his trip.

On the weekends, Uly often popped the hood on his '96 Ford to take care of it and keep it running. It was easy to work on, at least for him. And he could always find something to fix or clean.

When he moved to Albany, he found a house he could rent. It was in a quiet neighborhood.

The people were quiet.

The trains were not.

The railroad tracks were directly behind his house. And trains trundled by often enough.

Back on the road, Uly waved to all the other people driving trucks that he passed. He didn't know any of them, and they didn't know him. This was the thing about driving a truck that people who didn't drive trucks didn't know: when pickup truck drivers pass each other on the road, they give each other a friendly greeting. Uly didn't think much about it. It's what pickup truck drivers did.

When he got home, he carefully placed his keys and wallet on the end of the kitchen counter in the same place he always did so he wouldn't lose them. That was a hard-won habit.

The house was quiet. He thought for the thousandth time that he needed a dog. One of the guys at work had said his dog was about to have puppies. Uly didn't want to wait two more months for a tiny puppy. There was a perfect puppy at the pound, shelter, or whatever they called it here. He would make time to visit it after he returned from his trip.

He changed into a T-shirt and his favorite khaki cargo shorts and then leaned back in the big recliner he bought when he moved to Albany.

He grabbed the remote but paused as he pointed it at the TV. Uly sighed.

A feeling of being a little too alone hit him and he sighed again. There was a point at which "alone" became "lonely," and that point was easy to cross on a Friday night.

He missed Rachel. He regretted not having been better about staying in touch with her. She hadn't been supportive of him when he took this job.

She had a great job. Despite that, he never wanted her to pay for supper when they went out to eat. That would have been humiliating to him even though he knew it was old-fashioned. He always paid with his own money and never let on that he was frequently on the verge of being broke.

When he first moved to Albany, he took all the overtime he could get. He was normally exhausted when he got home. He hadn't called her often enough. Now, it seemed like she didn't want to talk to him anymore. He wasn't sure what to do. Maybe it was time to move on. She seemed to have.

He turned on the TV. A qualifying race of the International Superbike Grand Prix was on.

Perfect.

RACHEL
Friday Evening

Rachel watched as the waiter served all the dishes. She and her older brother, Robert, knew what to expect. Her friend from work, Ali, had never been to this diner before, and she was wide-eyed at the size of the servings.

Pancakes a foot wide extended beyond the sides of a huge platter; sausage patties the size of saucers, big plates of scrambled eggs, bowls of grits, fruit, orange juice, coffee, and all the extras filled the table for the three of them.

Ali shook her head and stared at the pancakes on the plate in front of her. "Rachel warned me!"

Rachel nodded. "Don't worry, if you can't eat it all, Robert will finish it off for you."

Robert looked up and nodded at Ali while chewing a mouthful of omelet.

Ali looked at the omelet. "That looks like you dumped a whole skillet of fajitas into a skillet full of fried eggs."

"Um, yeah. It's good!"

A couple from New York City had moved to Doraville and later opened a restaurant they named The Manhattan Diner. This was in the 1970s, and they had very little success.

They changed the name to Doraville Diner and started serving breakfast twenty-four hours a day, keeping the over-sized New York portions. Soon after that they added grits to the menu since they hated saying no to every person who walked through the door.

Naming the restaurant for the town and serving huge portions before it was fashionable made the Doraville Diner a local institution. It didn't hurt for them to be community oriented as well. A DeKalb County classic car club discovered they were welcome to use the restaurant's bigger-than-average parking lot for events. That had evolved to Friday night cruise-ins four or five times a year.

Robert never missed a cruise-in at the diner. He and a few friends had been taking their classic cars to local cruise-ins for years. Rachel had tagged along when she was younger and caught the bug. She loved that there was both a wide variety of vehicles that people brought to the events and a wide variety of people who brought them.

After high school, she went to college and eventually finished nursing school at Emory. While in school and during the first few years she worked, she didn't give much thought to cars because there was no time for it.

Since Emory was so close, she didn't move far from home. After completing her degree, she got a good job at a doctor's office in Decatur, in DeKalb County, and bought a house nearby at a time when houses were much less expensive than they had been a decade earlier.

Robert took a break from his omelet. "Talk to Uly lately, Rache?"

Rachel looked at Robert with a grimace. "Um. No."

"Oh. Okay. Is he still down in south Georgia?"

Ali smirked. "Yes. He's still down in Awl-binny?" She drawled with a questioning lilt, successfully making Rachel laugh at their inside joke. She turned to Robert to explain, "Uly said they don't say 'ahl-buh-nee' like Albany, New York. They say 'Awl-binny?' And they go up at the end like it's a question."

"Awl-binny?" Ali quipped again.

Robert laughed. "I don't think I know how I would say it."

Rachel had met Uly at a soccer World Cup viewing party a year-and-a-half earlier. They had talked and discovered they had lots of mutual friends and some mutual interests. Rachel invited him to join her a week later at a Doraville Diner cruise-in.

Uly asked Rachel out after that, so they went out a few times.

Rachel grew up in a community not far from downtown Atlanta in DeKalb County. Over a hundred languages were spoken by the mix of people and families who had settled there. She spoke a dialect of Spanish common to her mom's family and was proud of it. She allowed her English to have a touch of a Spanish accent. She could also intentionally dial

up various versions of Southern accents, shift back to Spanish, or skip over to a neutral Western American accent she
picked up while visiting Colorado. She didn't consider it fake
to switch accents. It was a tool in her social and workday tool-
box.

When it came to men in her life, Rachel's attitude was that
she wanted someone who wasn't afraid of a committed relationship. She found she could run off most losers by, first,
not giving them any money and, second, by inviting them to
church.

Uly had never asked for money and was undaunted by a
church-going girlfriend.

"I used to go with my grandparents, but I haven't been
to church in years, Rache. I don't even own a tie! What do I
wear?"

She put him at ease about the dress code. Over the months
they grew closer, but then he announced he might take a job
in south Georgia.

Rachel had worked for several years before meeting Uly
and had thought about buying a classic car. After he moved to
Albany, she was depressed. She was also angry at herself for
being depressed.

One day she called Robert. "Let's go shopping."

"Huh?"

"I said, 'Let's go shopping.' You drive."

For years, she had been looking at classics and talking to
their owners. She then researched and shopped online until

she knew what she wanted. All she needed to do was take a test drive and make a deal with the classic car dealership in the Atlanta area.

She could do her own basic maintenance, but more importantly she could talk the talk. She didn't need Robert to help her buy a car. What she needed was for him to give her a ride so she could drive her new car home.

She loved her new classic so much she gave it a name. She was also determined to drive it and enjoy it. She could see it in the parking lot of the Doraville Diner from the booth where she, her brother, and Ali were sitting.

A few people were standing around admiring it. She wanted to hurry up and finish eating so she could walk out there and tell everybody about her new baby—her Baby D.

LANCE
Friday Night

On a moonless night, stars filled the dark sky above an abandoned RV park and campground north of Savannah. Tent pads laid out near the back of the park were entirely overgrown. The old gravel parking pads were almost as bad. There were no cabins here but there was a small bathhouse. The roof had collapsed, and the water had been turned off for decades. The poles with outdoor security lights were still standing, although Lance had never seen the lights on.

He spoke in a mumbling rasp. "Partially, because it's important to understand the choices we make … that the choices … I choose this … " He trailed off in the darkness.

He felt he wasn't making the point exactly the way he wished. His voice had become a quiet rasp after decades of incessantly speaking aloud.

With thick fingers covered in grime and callouses, Lance fumbled around inside an old Piggly Wiggly grocery store buggy in search of something he felt he needed. Something was missing from his curated assortment of items, something he might need, something practical. He couldn't see the items in the buggy, but he knew all of them by touch.

"Not the point … " he muttered, trying to think while he searched.

The RV park had flooded one-too-many times when hurricanes had approached the area at high tide, so the property had been neglected and ignored for years. A few rotting and collapsing travel trailers still dotted the high brush. Lance was happy when he had found an RV nearly two decades earlier.

Back then, he had still been strong. He had recently left home for good. Years of exposure to the outdoors hadn't yet dragged him down. Once he found the RV park, he worked to make one of the abandoned travel trailers both possum and snake resistant and somewhat dry most of the time.

The grocery buggy was sitting outside, next to the RV, under a tattered blue tarp he had acquired. The buggy's rusting wire basket corralled a dank assortment of items he may or may not have used on a day-to-day basis.

A soft, unending *ak-rak ak-rak ak-rak* of thousands of katydids and annual cicadas rose from the forest of gnarled coastal pines all around him.

He practiced his argument, editing and correcting its content in his mind. "It's not that I don't have choices. The point is there are choices I don't know I don't have. Yep, yep." Lance was satisfied with that thought. Then he continued his incoherent muttering into the dark.

He continuously worked out the details of his argument by speaking aloud almost all the time. It had begun as an argument with his father when he left home the last time, angry and obsessed with trying to make his point.

Now it was something else: an endlessly iterative soliloquy or an evolving rationalization he imagined he might share with someone who questioned his reasoning with regard to his decisions. It had become a dissertation about dignity and individuality and choice and options.

It was genius.

It was also highly ironic because, while he didn't understand his own choices, he was occasionally aware of the choices other people faced.

He coughed a rasping, hacking, deep chest cough. He had been in denial about his coughing for years. "It's just mold."

He did feel better if he only slept in the RV a few hours at a time and didn't stay in it when he was awake.

He had already slept in the RV for a while that Friday night, like most nights for nearly twenty years. Lance didn't consider himself homeless. A squatter wasn't technically homeless.

He stopped fumbling around in the Piggly Wiggly buggy and sat in a chair he had found before continuing his ongoing commentary. "The key is to understand that a variety, that multiple options enhance liberty. Choice, therefore, is critical to the good life that—"

A blink.

An internal swirl.

A new reference—a memory—twisted out of the swirl.

He was aware of an insertion into his waking consciousness, a recollection of a memory that hadn't previously existed. It intruded and interrupted his theorizing about choice.

His brain created a short rhyme as a verbal, autonomous response to the new engram.

Jump back,

What do you lack?

Umbrella fella.

White Cadillac!

The words came to him, cementing the memory as the internal swirl evaporated, collapsing into time. The rhyme was not the actual engram itself.

Ak-rak, ak-rak, the cicadas didn't care.

He considered the interloping object of memory. It wasn't exactly a "vision." It included specific visuals along with an idea: in his mind's eye, an umbrella opened and then closed. He didn't recognize the man holding the umbrella. Next, the man opened the umbrella and closed it again. Behind the man in the distance, a classic Cadillac pulled up and parked in the open desert. The same man opened the passenger door and stepped out of the car.

The man. Hope. A journey.

That was all there was to the new memory.

Lance contemplated the meaning of all this without understanding. He didn't need to understand. The images and ideas in his memory would be relevant and practical in the future, but he didn't know the context or the exact timing.

This wasn't a new experience. He was used to being occasionally aware of the imminent choices of other people. His choices were another matter entirely.

Lance was patient. The new memory wasn't for this moment, in the dark, in the campground.

He continued talking out loud, practicing, editing, defining the ideas, following the logic, lecturing the katydids in the dark.

"—that the choices we make are reeling shadows cast by the best of us as we attempt to rise above a world where those of us having conviction that the tide once loosed will rebound, turning back upon itself, canceling its own advance."

He paused. "Yep, yep."

He tried not to think about it, but he was distracted by the new memory. The little rhyme was there, encapsulating the memory. He avoided repeating it so it wouldn't become an annoying lyrical thorn stuck in his brain.

He decided to get some more sleep. In the morning, the sun would rise, and he would go as he did every day to a favorite location that offered more shade than the RV campground. He needed the better protection it offered from the heat of the day and the stifling humidity.

ANT
Saturday Morning

Ant worked quickly, dropping food on the Waffle House's sizzling grill. "Antonio Toscanelli is my name, but it's not Italian."

Ant explained his heritage somewhat inaccurately, but he was busy cooking for the early Saturday morning crowd and was avoiding getting distracted. A long old scar ran from his temple to his chin and moved when he talked.

Jake, the young man sitting at the counter opposite the grill, nursed his coffee while he waited for Ant to finish cooking his breakfast.

"Sounds Italian, is all I'm saying."

"But do I sound Italian?"

"You sound like you just got done muddin' in a monster truck."

Ant wasn't paying Jake much attention. "I'll take that as a compliment."

"But you also look Italian."

"Actually, I just got done with your 'taters."

Ant was a magnet for argumentative people who didn't have much to argue about. He always, without fail, engaged in back-and-forth banter with them no matter what they said.

He was already plating up food for other customers. A waitress efficiently slipped by without a word and picked up the plate of fried hash browns from the boards next to the grill where Ant was working. She gave it to Jake with the rest of his breakfast while doing four other things as she walked by.

Jake, undaunted by futility, corrected Ant. "You mean you're done with my 'scattered.'"

"No, I'm done with your 'drop.' Your drop was 'scattered,' but it was still a 'drop.'"

Jake shrugged, not knowing what a "drop" was.

"I could confuse you with more Waffle House Advanced Grill Operator Lingo, but it wouldn't make your breakfast any more delightful than I have already made it. *Capisce?*"

Jake couldn't help himself. "'Toscanelli' sounds Italian is all I'm saying.'"

"My name is Italian, but I'm not."

"That's what I'm saying. Your name is Italian."

"I grew up right here in Dublin, Georgia. My family has been here, like, five generations."

"But you could be Italian again. They let you do that there."

Ant said good morning to his replacement, another cook who stepped in next to him at the grill.

"A'ight, Jake, enjoy your breakfast, buddy."

He walked through the front door with his part of the tips, relieved to finally be off work. Ant had been working eight hours since ten o'clock Friday evening. Now, he would go home, get a shower, and sleep about six hours. Then he would get up, get ready, and go to work at his other job as a cook in the restaurant at Merlie's Truck Stop, his aunt and uncle's business.

He would leave work at Merlie's in the evening wearing his Waffle House uniform and go to work at Waffle House. He did that six days a week—every day except Sunday. It made for a long week, but it was what he had to do to both pay the bills and build up a good nest egg.

He took a big breath of fresh air and noted that even at six in the morning the light breeze had a warmth that warned of a hot day in the making.

He sat down in his '94 Toyota pickup and felt the relief in his lower back. He was used to walking on concrete floors all day, but it was wearing him out.

He backed out of his parking space. Ant couldn't see if any other cars were approaching from his left or right because his view was blocked on both sides by what passed these days for normal-sized trucks. Either one of them could have successfully run over and crushed a small division of German Panzers.

He wished he could afford to get rid of his little truck and buy a real one like those parked beside him, but he refused to go into debt. He could sell his Toyota for good money and quit one of his day jobs for a year. Of course, then he would need to buy another car so he would have a ride, and that would mean going into debt or buying something used with unknown problems. He felt better about dealing with the known problems he already had.

Life was often a series of catch-22s like that. At some point he had decided to trust in Jesus and be happy with what he had.

He thought of his recent conversation with his fiancée, Nancy. "People have to decide they have enough," he had said.

She considered this. "You mean they have enough stuff?"

"Yes, but also enough of other things that aren't things. That they have enough of the more intangible aspects of life too."

"So, you're happy because you've decided you have enough?"

He looked at her, considering whether what she said was the way he felt. "I'm not unhappy."

"Then why not say 'I am happy?'" she challenged.

"I enjoy the work I do, and I like helping people. Truth is, there are things I want in life I don't have."

"Thing-things?"

"Yes," he admitted.

"Intangible things?"

"No. I've got your love. That's the only intangible I want!"

"You're full of it, you know that?"

Ant was committed to helping people like the employees

at the Waffle House or at his aunt and uncle's truck stop. People with jobs were often the people who needed the most help. If not them, then someone they were serving a meal to often needed help to make it to whatever was next for them.

He had explained this to his friends one evening when they were all at his place grilling out. "People with real needs drop in all the time looking for nothing more than a cheap cup of coffee."

Ant had the cooking skills, but he only owned a modest charcoal grill. His house was small with practically no place for people to gather. That didn't matter. They always ended up congregating at his house.

He was sitting there with his friends, letting the burgers and hotdogs cook. "None of us are hurting for anything."

One of Nancy's friends gave him a skeptical look. "Speak for yourself, Ant."

"No, I don't mean we don't work hard to make ends meet. I mean we make ends meet and have places to live."

One of his buddies jumped in. "I know what you mean, dude, since I'm independently wealthy and all like you To-scanellis!"

Ant ignored the remark, which wasn't true. "We should start a fund. You know? Something for people who are passing through and need help."

He looked around at his friends. "I don't know how, but we can come up with something."

Nancy considered his idea. "So, something bigger than

just us helping people when we can? Maybe Dr. Chuck would know how to start something like that."

That had been over a year ago. Some of his friends and many of his family members worked in food service in one way or another. Working together, they started helping people in the community or people who were passing through. Mostly it was travelers in need that people in food service met during the normal course of a day at work. Usually, some cash, a hot meal, or a ride someplace was all they needed.

Their small fund hadn't been much to worry about at first, and then that changed. As more of Ant's friends gave to the informal charity they had created, the increasing amount of money became something they needed to manage with more accountability.

Dr. Chuck wasn't a medical doctor. He had a doctorate in divinity and had been a pastor for forty years before he retired. Now, on Sundays, he normally attended a worship service at the retirement community where he lived. Ant's friends all knew him because he had either been their pastor or because he ventured out as much as four or five times a week to eat at local restaurants, including Merlie's and Waffle House.

Ant approached Dr. Chuck and discovered they could donate into and, when needed, access an existing indigent charity fund through the local ministerial association. Dr. Chuck invited Ant to speak to the pastors at one of their meetings. Ant pitched the idea to them, and they immediately agreed to help him work out the details.

RUSTY
Saturday Morning

Late Saturday morning Rusty was pressure washing his semitruck on the gravel driveway of his warehouse. Pressure washing a big rig was a chore for one person, but it had to be done because he had a busy week ahead.

Movement at Rusty's house next door caught his eye. His wife, Meg, was saying something to him from the back porch. She always did that—talking to him as if he could hear her when she knew he couldn't.

The gas-powered engine on the pressure washer drowned out all other sounds. He let go of the trigger on the long-handled nozzle, but that didn't help much. The pressure washer motor continued making as much noise as it had been.

He walked over to turn it off while Meg was still talking.

Meg finished in the sudden silence. "—to bring them a new three-door refrigerator."

"Yeah, I can call them to get the details."

He wondered who he was going to call.

"You're working too hard. Look at you."

"It's not sweat. It's just water blowing back."

It was mostly sweat.

He was a big guy, but he had gotten bigger in the last year or so, and he could tell. So could Meg.

Meg turned to go back to the house. "Merlie's down in Dublin," she stated flatly, offering the name of the caller without him needing to ask.

"Ant?"

"No. Merlie herself called."

It made no difference if he complained about not being able to hear her, or asked her to make sure he could hear, or didn't know what she was talking about.

They had been in sixth grade together. She and her friends could read lips, so the girls could talk in class without making any noise that drew a rebuke from teachers. Meg had assumed on the first day she met Rusty that he could read lips with no trouble at all. He had tried to explain then, and for the next decade, that neither he nor any of his buddies could read lips.

He eventually gave up and worked it out on a case-by-case basis. Meg would repeat herself sooner or later without prompting.

He had Merlie's number and made the call.

"Merlie?"

"Hey, Rusty. You've got our coffeemaker and everything, right?"

"Yeah."

"Do you have room on your truck for a three-door reach-in refrigerator when you come down next week?"

"I can make room."

The trailer was full of large boxes of paper supplies, cleaning products, and several big coffeemakers, all for different stops. He put some boxes intended for his first stops in the sleeper unit, and then he would deliver those items before he needed to use it.

"You don't have one in your warehouse, do you?"

"No. Nothing that big."

"Our walk-in fridge is too far from the wait station, and it's not set up for storage of single servings. That two-door fridge in the wait station quit on us. It's been too small for a long time. I don't want to pay to fix it when what we really need is a bigger one. You know? Why waste money on Band-Aids that aren't what we need when we can get the right thing now and not buy something twice?"

She reminded Rusty of her nephew, Ant. She would keep talking unless he interrupted. "So, you want a three-door reach-in refrigerator on casters, right? With glass doors?"

"Yes. I think you've seen our old two-door one in there. I'll email you the model number for the one I want."

"I can get it to you Monday if you need me to make a special run."

"No. You weren't planning to be here until Wednesday, were you? We can hold out until then."

"I'll take your old one and recycle it if you want me to."

They worked out a deal, but Rusty didn't know what it would cost exactly. Merlie trusted him.

He and Meg had settled in Chattanooga, Tennessee, near the Georgia state line. He had clients all over the Southeast and would go anywhere business took him.

He thought about where to get the refrigerator. He could stop in Atlanta or maybe get a better deal in Gainesville, but that was out of the way—over hill and dale through a chunk of north Georgia mountains. There were plenty of other vendors in the Atlanta area, which was a short ride down the road from Chattanooga in long-haul truck terms.

He finished cleaning up the bumper and tires. Then he climbed into the cab, backed up to the trailer, and connected the two.

Patting his old trailer on the side, he headed to the house.

The whole rig was his.

Or, rather, it belonged to Russel Adams Food Service Supplies & Equipment, Inc. Being a fully incorporated company was a hassle, but it worked out fine for him since Meg was the one who knew how to take care of all those details.

He and Meg owned all the shares of the company. She did the books, answered the phone, and handled advertising when she wasn't doing the same thing for a brewpub downtown.

He drove and moved stuff: big equipment but not enormous. Anything bigger than a commercial oven or three-door refrigerator would be too much for a one-man show. Not that he could lift anything that big by hand, but he had a motorized, hydraulic hand truck that took care of the heavy lifting.

A seventy-two-inch-wide refrigerator for Merlie wasn't too big, but he hoped Ant would be there when he started trying to install it. There was no doubt they would have to move something heavy at the truck stop to get this new, larger refrigerator where it needed to be.

His company provided commercial food-service supplies and equipment to restaurants, churches, office buildings, schools, and occasionally private homeowners with fancy kitchens. All kinds of places you wouldn't expect had commercial appliances for one reason or another. They needed new equipment regularly and supplies constantly.

He was also the most skilled truck driver he knew, which was saying something. It was true, but he didn't boast about it to anyone or act arrogant.

He could get his truck into and out of the tightest driveways and back alleys with his trailer fully loaded. He could back down a rutted mud path on the side of a mountain. He had done it. Once.

Of course, he didn't mind hauling anything his tractor could pull, but most of the time he limited it to core items he stocked or specialty products related to his normal business. Most companies couldn't deliver appliances on short notice.

Next-day appliance delivery put him in a class by himself. He would scramble to give next-day service to practically any customer in the Southeast. Having a niche was the key. He wasn't afraid to ask a premium price for a premium service, but he would work with a customer who had to have something they couldn't afford to help them get what they needed in a way that fit their budget.

He delivered and installed anything anywhere. Most commercial appliance vendors had panel trucks they used to make a quick trip with one item after their customer waited three weeks for them to get it into their warehouse.

Other companies had immense long-nosed sleeper-cab tractors and trailers so long they couldn't deliver to tight locations the way he could.

Rusty's truck was a short, snub-nosed cab-over 1990 Mack semitruck without a sleeper unit. He had bought it with cash at an auction years ago for much less than it was worth to him. It was a rough ride because the tractor itself was so short, but he had gotten used to it because it was exactly what he wanted and needed. He had cleaned, restored, or replaced every single part—or at least most of them—himself with some help from a local truck mechanic.

Behind the tractor, he pulled a twenty-eight-foot trailer with a reinforced undercarriage. This short rig gave him all the options he needed and few inconveniences.

Meg helped him design a small sleeper unit at the front of

the trailer. This was the same location food-service vendors normally installed a refrigerator-freezer section.

He bought all the parts for his sleeper unit from a local RV parts dealer, including a roof-mounted air conditioner. Six feet back from the front of the trailer, he installed a bulkhead with metal studs and aluminum panels and then installed the tiny homemade sleeper unit with a queen-size Murphy bed. Inside the cargo section of the trailer, behind the sleeper unit, he built a workbench with bins that could be secured for traveling. He had all the tools and everything he needed for appliance installations, truck repairs, or anything else he might need to do on the road.

This left more than twenty feet in the back of the trailer for hauling his customers' purchases. If he had been a mere broker and had to pay shipping to someone else, the whole business model would not have worked. Doing the deliveries himself saved him money on shipping and staying overnight in the trailer's sleeper unit saved on his travel costs.

Meg sometimes rode with him. Typically, that was only when it was time to hit the road for a vacation—they both refused to fly. He would park her bright-yellow convertible 2007 Saturn Sky roadster in the trailer and off they'd go.

He walked through the backyard and went into the house through the mudroom. While he washed his hands at the sink there, Meg was setting the table for lunch. She started talking to him. This time, he could hear her.

"Rusty, I called Juanita."

Juanita and her family owned one of the commercial food-service equipment stores in the Atlanta area.

"She has one of those refrigerators at their Marietta location for you."

Meg was pure gold. He didn't have anything to complain about.

MARTI
Saturday Noon

Marti checked her watch. It was almost time to start choir practice.

Her father was on his way from Dublin to her family's house on Tybee Island. It would take him at least two and a half hours to make the trip. He had called her before he left, so she still had plenty of time for the special choir practice she had called for today and would get home before he got there.

Meanwhile, she had work to do.

It was quiet inside the church sanctuary where Marti was organizing supplies they would need for their trip.

Though the overhead lights were off, it wasn't dark in the sanctuary of the Methodist church building here in historic downtown Savannah where she and Ted, her husband, and their children were members.

The building was historic; the congregation wasn't.

Often, congregations found maintaining a two-hundred-year-old building, keeping basic ministries going, and paying a pastor was difficult. As congregations aged, churches started losing too many members, youth pastors moved on and were not replaced, and families started going elsewhere. Visitors didn't end up joining. It was a vicious cycle.

Five years earlier their congregation of a few families had been meeting in a rented location usually used for a retail store. They were a church without an adequate building.

The building they were in now had been a church without a congregation after the last few elderly members decided they had to close the doors and sell.

Marti's church had worked hard to renovate the old church building and started growing by being friendly and welcoming.

She was paid a stipend to direct a traveling choir based out of her church. It wasn't the regular worship choir, which had its own director. Instead, this was a mission of the church. They supported other churches by attending their Sunday morning worship services and offering special music. Any church could book them and many had.

In fact, it was crazy how busy they had gotten. They had started with an occasional weekend three years earlier, but now they were booked every other weekend for two reasons: first, pastors, music directors, and congregations loved having visitors provide special music; and second, Marti's group was good!

Word had spread in Savannah and Chatham County and then to surrounding areas about a fantastic new gospel choir. They traveled at least one weekend a month. Sometimes they visited several churches in one month—but always on Sundays.

This was the first time they were planning to be gone overnight. It was much harder to schedule because most of the members worked weekdays.

She heard a few choir members starting to file into the practice room down a hall behind the sanctuary.

Marti finished organizing her supplies and exited the sanctuary through a door behind the choir loft. She walked down to the choir room. The group was mostly all there.

"Y'all are right on time and so dependable. Thank you! Once everyone gets here, we'll go through all the songs we're singing and then load up the trailer."

Marti listened to the chatter of choir members entering and getting settled.

Becky asked about her dad. "Is Dr. Chuck going to be able to stay with the kids like you'd hoped, Marti?"

"Yes. He's on the road as we speak."

"That's good."

"It's not like my big kids need a babysitter. But Dad loves to visit, and he's a big help if Ted has to work late."

Their accompanist arrived in a flurry and sat down at the piano to get his music in place.

Marti had grown up singing in the church. Now she sang with the group and would occasionally step forward to be the lead voice on songs with the choir backing her up.

She only stood in front and directed when they were learning new music. She had added a few new songs for this trip, which helped to keep the choir from getting bored. In many ways this was a greatest-hits tour. They were doing all their favorite gospel music pieces; as well as some older, more formal arrangements; and a few contemporary Christian songs.

After the whole choir arrived, she turned on her director's voice. "So, is everyone able to take off from work Monday and Tuesday?"

They all affirmed they were going to be there. That was good news. It was a big trip.

Typically, they traveled twice a month on Sunday mornings to churches all around southeast Georgia that weren't more than a hundred miles away. They would perform at a host church and then drive home. They practiced on Tuesday evenings while the regular church choir practiced on Wednesday evenings.

This trip was for a revival service at a church in Charleston, South Carolina. The host church was planning to hold an old-fashioned, camp-meeting-style four-day revival beginning with the Sunday morning worship service and then another one Sunday night and two more each day at noon and six p.m. through Wednesday.

Marti's travel choir would only be there from Sunday evening until Tuesday evening. The host church would be taking care of the music for the Sunday morning service and the Wednesday services.

Marti flipped through her music binder, still not sure which songs to sing for each service in the coming week. She decided she still needed to pray about it.

"OK, y'all, let's warm up."

CHUCK
Saturday Afternoon

"I love this couch," said Chuck.

"I know. It was Mom's."

Marti had gotten home from choir practice before her dad arrived. Now she was standing in the kitchen behind Chuck.

Chuck nodded. "M-hm. But I always have liked it because it's comfortable." Chuck ran his hand across the dark-mocha leather with a distant look on his face. "This is real leather. The whole thing."

"None of that fake vinyl stuff for y'all back then, huh, Dad?" Marti wasn't mocking him, but she was having a little fun at his expense.

He turned and looked back at his daughter with a good-natured, overly dramatic, accusative glare. "You stole my line."

Marti adopted a tone of casual frankness. "I have all your lines memorized."

She put on her yard shoes at the back door then opened it. Chuck could hear the distant voices of his grandchildren in the backyard. They were returning from fishing in the marshes between Tybee Island and the mainland.

"Oh yeah? Well, what am I about to say next?"

"The kids are back from fishing."

He scowled. "How did you know—" but the door clicked shut behind Marti.

Sue's sofa faced a huge bank of windows in the living room. Chuck sat and looked out at the expanse of blue sky that started above a line of distant trees. He watched for movement in the marsh. Narrow, sunlit lanes of water undulated through the tall grasses of the saltwater marsh that extended from the edge of the backyard to the tree line miles away. Trees didn't grow in the marsh itself. Instead, they were on the distant mainland banks.

He continued to study the water. Sometimes a big fish or a dolphin would move the surface, but he didn't see anything like that today.

From this vantage point, he couldn't see the dock where the kids tied up the boat. The house was on stilts the way many coastal homes are built. The TV was off and everything was quiet except for some soft bumps under the house as the kids stored their fishing and paddling gear. Though lights were off in the house, it was well lit by the ambient light of the bright outdoors.

The house was also meat-locker cool. Chuck pulled a colorful afghan Sue had crocheted years ago over his legs and sat there enjoying what remained of the calm quiet before the kids came in.

He had sat on that sofa forty years or more. It was almost as old as his daughter. Marti, his youngest, had been born when he was in his forties himself. He reckoned he had always been old to her.

The sofa was built like a tank and had only gotten better with age. It had been what his wife, Sue, had wanted, so he bought it. She didn't ask for much, but she could have expensive tastes. Nine hundred 1980s dollars! For a couch! It had been emotionally traumatic to spend that much on a couch. He had lost a few nights' sleep over it until he decided to move on. Later he decided it had been worth it. It was extra long and could easily seat four or five people.

But things had changed.

Sue's couch didn't fit in his little apartment at the "nursing home" in Dublin where he lived now ... now that Sue had passed away, and he had moved from their fifty-acre homestead of mostly untouched forest.

He remembered that day over two years earlier when Marti had tried to explain why she wanted him to move.

"It's not a 'nursing home,' Dad. It's an 'assisted-living facility.' It's nice. You can come and go as you like, and nobody is going to 'spy' on you."

Chuck was purposefully obstinate. "I can remember to take my own pills without some nurse nagging me."

"Nobody is checking on you and giving you your meds. It's not a nursing home. And the whole place is on one level with no stairs or steps to navigate. There's hardly a step-up on the whole campus."

Chuck knew Marti had been frustrated with him and had tried to hide it. He also knew she wondered how many times he had fallen when he was going in and out the front door of their family's old farmhouse out in the middle of nowhere.

"Well, if they can't be bothered to check on me or give me my pills, then why can't I just stay right here? I know where things are here, and I know the neighbors. I love this house."

"Lawd! Dad, how many times do I have to go over—"

"Don't 'Lawd' me!"

"You won't have to fix the roof, you won't have to cook, you won't have to climb the stairs—"

"The roof don't need fixin', and I eat at Merlie's most days."

And I don't ever go upstairs anymore, he added silently, but he knew better than to say it out loud and open that can of worms with his daughter.

"What if a tree falls on a power line out here in the boonies?"

"I could buy a generator."

"M-hm." She continued her argument. "You won't have to cut all that grass, clean the house, or, worse yet, fall without anybody knowing."

He was indignant. "I'm careful. I'm not gonna fall."

He was also lying. He had fallen more times than he was telling. And as for cleaning the house, he didn't think he needed to clean anything since he never got anything dirty.

Marti added, "And you don't like your neighbors."

"Well, I ain't moving to some hurricane-magnet island in the swamps."

It was true, he didn't like the neighbors. Not that he disliked them. Longleaf pine trees were the only neighbors across the road. Neighbors on both sides were so far away he wouldn't recognize their cars. None of his church friends lived near him and too many of his other friends had passed away.

"I'm not trying to move you to Tybee Island with us. You can stay right here in Dublin. Why do you always say that?"

He called the area a "hurricane magnet" because he would rather live on Tybee Island with his daughter and son-in-law and, more importantly, his three grandkids.

His goal was to say he *did not* want to live there in a way Marti would believe. He didn't want to impose on her or Ted or the kids. There wasn't room for him in their house on Tybee Island—which, at any rate, had more steps than a lighthouse—and there was no way he would be able to talk them into moving back to Dublin.

The kids loved the island. Mike and Gabe, his fifteen-year-old identical-twin grandsons had a johnboat their parents had given them on their eighth birthday. They took it out on the marsh where they fished almost daily. Most of the time they took Tabitha, his twelve-year-old granddaughter, as well.

I'm just glad they don't have their noses in their fool phones all day.

The kids burst through the back door, shattering his silent thoughts.

"How was the swamp fishin', boys and girls?"

Mike and Gabe spoke in unison, "It's a 'marsh,' Pop." They didn't do that all the time, but it happened.

Marti jumped in, "Looks like a swamp to me."

"That's Pop's line. And I'm the only girl," Tabitha said, correcting them both.

Mike disappeared upstairs and Gabe went to the refrigerator. He opened the door, dug around under tin foil over a plate, and pulled out a hunk of cold roast beef. Amazingly, in spite of the boys' appetites, a third of it had survived to be refrigerated.

Talking and chewing with his mouth full, Gabe said, "Tabitha was the only one who caught anything. What's for supper?"

"Y'all get ready. Pop wants to eat on River Street, and Daddy's going to meet us there."

The kids went upstairs to get ready without having to be told more than once.

Chuck looked back at Marti in the kitchen. "Why did you have to go outside when they got back from fishing?"

"Because they don't put up their gear, they don't tie up the boat, and they don't throw the fish back or bother to clean them."

Marti walked around the island in the kitchen to join her dad in the living room and plopped down next to him on the couch. "And then the dead fish stink to high heaven. And too often they make sure their sister 'accidentally' falls into the marsh while getting out of the boat."

"So you have to go see about them tying up the boat?"

"Yes, but I do at least get them to hose off their nasty feet and legs before they walk into my house and leave marsh mud on everything."

"Where's Tabitha's fish?"

"The rule is 'you clean what you catch,' and Tabitha usually throws hers back to avoid the hassle of cleaning them."

"Too squeamish?"

Tabitha was walking back into the living room. "No."

She always cleaned up and got ready at the speed of light and only ever wore the simplest summer T-shirt and shorts. She sat down on the other side of Pop. "My fish was too small, and it was too hot today to catch much of anything, but Mike and Gabe just like to go out in the boat."

Chuck thought that was sweet. "They like to take you fishing?"

Tabitha was matter-of-fact, "No, they like to leave me at the house." She didn't offer any further explanation.

Marti looked at her dad. "The boys want you to drive your car to the restaurant."

Mike spoke from the stairs. "Down River Street."

Then he joined them on the couch.

"Slowly," Gabe yelled from his room upstairs.

"Can I sit on the back wearing a tiara with my legs crossed

daintily and wave like a princess?" Tabitha never pretended to be a princess, but she did like to practice being sarcastic.

Chuck stood for the first time in a while. His knees creaked as he got up. "Of course, Tabitha. Anything you want."

An hour later Ted, Chuck's son-in-law, met them at the restaurant. The boys sat on either side of their grandfather, and Tabitha sat across from him between her parents. They were finishing off an appetizer plate of fried calamari and waiting for their entrées to be served.

Mike leaned toward Chuck. "You should go out on the boat with us, Pop."

Gabe agreed. "Yeah, a bunch of times."

Chuck wanted to join them. "M-hm. Let's do that one day while I'm here."

Marti had been quietly watching her dad chat with her children. She waited for them to finish. "Thanks for helping with the kids this week, Dad."

He looked up and caught her eye. "How was choir practice?"

"It was great. My group of singers is an embarrassment of riches. The travel choir has the best singers in the church. We had hoped this would be an ensemble from within the chancel choir—"

"Y'all still use that word. I thought 'chancel' was a Methodist word."

"No, Dad. It's a church-building word for the area where ... you know, the choir and pulpit area. We travel so much and practice on a different day of the week. So it's just too much for some people to be in both choirs."

Chuck knew where this was going. "And the best singers are in the travel choir, so that has caused hurt feelings between you and the chancel choir."

Marti nodded and frowned while chewing calamari. "Not just me. The whole travel choir feels it. The regular choir members are either jealous or feel like they're second fiddle."

Ted shook his head. "And what's silly about that is they're a great choir." He meant it.

Marti tried not to roll her eyes. "Well, the travel choir has been drawing the best singers. In some cases, our practice time fits their schedule better."

Chuck looked at his daughter. Out of habit his voice took on some of the timbre of the old preacher in him. "Sometimes God frustrates our relationships on purpose to get us to be reflective about our own ... " He paused, trying to be diplomatic.

Marti finished the sentence for him. "'Pride,' Dad?"

"I was going to say 'perspective.'"

She looked at him, smirking. "M-hm."

LUCY
Sunday Morning

Lucy MacAllister didn't always wear a hat to church. It was a lady's prerogative. She could surprise and delight with a fine hat or not. She could still hear her mother repeating her rules for girls. "Lucille, a young lady should strive to surprise and delight her host without any attendant undue scandal for her audience."

Lucy smiled. She was pushing a hundred years old and still had no idea what all that meant. She was pretty sure that for most of her life she had surprised without delighting. Likewise, anyone who was scandalized was probably past due getting their boat rocked.

Lucy had attended the Susannah Wesley Sunday School class that morning and was making her way down a wide hallway to the sanctuary to attend the worship service.

Doris, her perennial bridge and Sunday morning pew partner slipped up beside her. "You sure are smiling big this morning, Luce. Kill another cat?"

"Shut up. I don't kill cats."

"You just celebrate their demise."

"I don't celebrate death. I simply appreciate the emergence of order from chaos."

From a side door off the hallway, they entered the narthex, a wide-open space between the front doors and the entrance into the sanctuary.

The ladies stopped and looked into the room. People making their way into the church were welcomed by a young couple wearing badges that said "Greeter."

Lucy leaned toward Doris while looking at the greeters. "Is that couple new or have we met them? I don't remember."

"How do you define 'new'?"

Then Lucy remembered their names. "The Kicklighters."

"Yes."

In previous years they would have walked arm-in-arm into the sanctuary, but Lucy's rollator prevented it these days. They settled for walking in together.

Ushers at all doors were handing out folded paper bulletins with the order of worship in them.

Lucy looked at Doris. "One day—"

"We are going to ask to be ushered to our seat."

Lucy shook her head in mock disapproval. "They don't actually usher."

"Please don't complain to the pastor about it. Again."

"He knew I was joking."

"I don't think so."

Unless she was too under the weather, Lucy attended church every Sunday morning without missing one. Although she had missed many Sundays when she and Roanoke, her husband, had been running their bed-and-breakfast.

As they made their way down the aisle to their pew, Lucy could see that a family with children was occupying at least half of it.

They stopped. Lucy whispered, "What about that family, Dor? Are they new?"

"Yes. Definitely."

"I don't think they know that's our pew."

Lucy and Doris were friendly and chatted with the new family and then settled into their places.

Suddenly the organist began playing the prelude at a heart-stopping volume.

Lucy looked around to see what attendance would be like this morning. More people filed in, leaving the front pews empty, but it looked like it would be a good crowd.

She was thankful for friends and family—though they lived farther away than she liked—and thankful her church was a vibrant place that welcomed and ministered to both young families and elderly widows like herself.

Over the decades, she had often told guests at the bed-and-breakfast they would be welcome at this church if they wished to visit one while staying in Charleston. Many had accepted her offer.

As she sat listening to the complicated arrangement of

classical church music coming from the organ, she watched the acolytes light the candles.

She was also thankful the guitar players and drummers had their own separate worship service. She loved the people who went to those services and the ones who played the music, but she liked the traditional hymns and organ music she was used to for church, especially on Sunday morning.

Doris leaned over and spoke loud enough for Lucy to hear. "Those revival services start tonight over there where Cathleen goes to church."

Lucy looked at her. "You want to go check out that gospel choir she was going on about?"

"Pick you up at five?"

"Hat or no hat?"

"It'll be crowded."

Lucy wasn't sure about getting back out on the town tonight, but she didn't have time to respond because the music ended and the pastor stood up. "Good morning!"

ULY
Sunday Morning

Uly's eyes snapped open late Sunday morning.

What time is it? Oh no! My work clothes are dirty!

He jumped up and rushed around, tripping over his own feet looking for clothes he might need to pack for his trip.

He smelled something. His work clothes reeked. He threw the clothes he would need for his trip into the washing machine.

The washer was older than his truck and grimy around the lid. He suspected a previous occupant had donated the washer and a matching dryer to the house long after both were past their prime.

He stuffed the tub full and dumped washing powder on the clothes. Then he added more in hopes of killing the smell.

He turned the big wash-cycle knob to the Heavy setting and the Wash/Rinse temperature dial to Hot/Cold. Then he pulled the knob out to start the machine. Water started filling the tub.

Good. He was not running late. He still had time to wash,

dry, and pack his clothes before he had to leave, but it would be close.

He ran to take a shower, shave, and get what he needed together to leave for Savannah. After the shower, he dressed in cargo shorts, T-shirt, and tennis shoes since he wanted to wear something casual for the long ride from Albany to Savannah.

He thought about his preparations for the trip. The ten-dollar bill was in his wallet, so he had some snack money, but that was all. Thankfully, he wouldn't need extra money since the company was covering food and lodging.

He looked at his wallet. Rachel had given it to him for Christmas. He liked the rich, brown leather. Inside, he kept it simple and slim. No credit cards bulked up the size of his wallet—at least not anymore.

He had learned to manage debt through a program at Rachel's church. They didn't say not to have a credit card, but he had worked to pay his off. He was happier that way. Of course, it wasn't using a credit card that was the problem—it was compounding interest on debt that never got paid down that killed your paycheck every month.

He knew some people wanted a credit card as a safety net. That was fine for them, but he was used to not living with one.

He had a debit card he needed to activate laying around the house somewhere. That was exactly like a credit card, so it could potentially be a good enough safety net for him if he truly needed it.

He reminded himself again to find it and activate it.

He stared at his wallet. Something was wrong. He held it in his hand, thinking hard.

When was the last time he had seen that bright-yellow memo from Joe?

Had he dropped it at the gas station? Yes, but he had picked it up and put it back in his pocket. He checked the kitchen counter. Nothing. He checked the recliner, the side tables in the living room, and pawed through clutter on the dining room table.

He went to his bedroom and looked on the floor where his dirty clothes had been. He stopped and stood quietly because now he remembered where the memo was.

Suddenly it sounded like a train crashed through his laundry room.

He ran back to the other end of the house where the washing machine was banging against the dryer and pounding against the wall. It shook the whole house as it furiously slammed itself from side to side. Despite being tethered by a water hose and a power cord, it was walking itself toward the back door, making a break for freedom.

Uly slapped the wash-cycle knob to turn off the machine. He opened the lid and grabbed heavy, wet pants and shirts. He pulled them up out of the tub. As he already suspected, bright-yellow pieces of wet paper were stuck all over his clothes.

The memo had been full of common sense stuff anyway; it didn't matter now.

He pushed his clothes back into the tub, rearranging them and trying to balance the load. He started the washer again right where it sat in the middle of the laundry room. For an achingly long minute it turned slowly, gradually spinning faster and faster until it was up to speed.

It was mostly balanced now, and it was a blessing he didn't have to try to balance the load a second time. He walked away to let it complete the rinse and spin cycles.

He absently straightened up the house while waiting for the washing machine to finish. He tried to remember anything he might have read on the memo besides the departure time.

He walked back into the laundry room just as the washer wound down it's spin cycle. As soon as it stopped, he pulled out his wet clothes littered with yellow bits of paper.

He threw everything into the dryer and set the timer for thirty minutes on the hottest setting and scooted the now empty washer back into its place. Then he went in search of two duffel bags. He found them, packed his toiletries, and made sure he had his keys, an ink pen, his phone, and his wallet.

As soon as the clothes were close enough to dry, he would stuff everything into the duffel bags and then rush out the door. When he got to work, he would be early and would look like he was on top of things.

Having slept through breakfast, he grabbed some cold, leftover pizza and munched on it for lunch. Then a loud, insistent buzzing jangled his nerves when the dryer finished.

Uly packed his clothes, turned off lights in the house, locked the door, and jumped into his truck. There was no hurry. It took ten minutes to get to the office, and he had at least twenty. He expected to be the first one there.

Uly parked in the employee parking area beside the old farmhouse-turned-office building. Joe and two other men drove around to meet him in a new four-wheel-drive truck with a full-size crew cab and the company logo on the front doors.

"Uly, where have you been?"

"I thought I was early, Joe."

"You're late. My memo said to be here at one-thirty to pack the truck."

"I thought it said 'departing no later than two.'"

"At least you read that much. It don't matter. We took care of it. Just get in."

"Yes, sir."

"Alrighty then. Let's go."

Joe didn't seem upset. That was good.

They hit the road and drove a few hours.

Joe, Uly, and the other guys talked and laughed like old friends. Joe explained the plan for meals. "We're stopping in Hawkinsville to buy ice, and then we're going to a butcher shop. That's what I usually do."

In Hawkinsville, they stopped to buy twenty-pound bags of ice. While the ice machine worked, Joe got Uly's attention and patted the side of a big, clean but well used gas grill loaded on the back of the truck. "We grill out every night. It's more fun than eating junk food all week. I like to have real food for real men. That's what I always say!"

"Yeah, Joe. That's a nice grill. Propane too. Looking forward to it."

Once all the bags were full, they dumped the ice in large coolers.

Then they crossed the river and turned down a side road to go to Harris Kuntry Meats, a butcher shop. When they stopped again, everyone went inside.

The store was nice and included a good variety of other grocery items. Customers were lined up waiting to order from the counter. One of the butchers working there recognized Joe when he walked in and waved him over to one side. "Joe, I've got you ready."

He pushed a hand truck stacked with boxes out from the back storage area of the store. It looked like Joe had ordered an entire cow.

He took the hand truck. "Thanks, Drew."

Drew glanced at Uly.

"Drew, we've got a new member of the team. This is Uly."

Drew nodded. "Nice to meet you."

"Hi, Drew. Nice place."

"Don't let these old boys get the best of you, Uly."

"I won't," Uly said, and they all laughed.

The other men had been shopping. They had corn on the cob for grilling, all kinds of other vegetables, and a cart filled with more food and supplies.

Joe pulled out a round wad of money and peeled off a stack of twenty-dollar bills to pay for the steaks, sausages, chicken, and the other groceries.

At the truck, they unboxed everything and dumped the groceries in the coolers. Then they continued on back roads to the interstate on the way to Savannah.

Three hours after picking up their groceries, Joe pulled off the interstate and drove into the parking lot of a small hotel north of Savannah. He checked Uly and one crew member into a room with two double beds. Joe and the other man each got their own room.

Joe was the boss, so he had a room to himself. No big deal. Made sense. Uly was happy to be there, and he knew deep down that he was going to get a special blessing from this experience.

A while later, Joe went around to the rooms and asked the men to help him move the big grill off the truck to a small patio with a picnic table.

Joe fired it up and one of the guys appeared with a huge box of marinated steaks. He had some other meats, vegetables, and spices with him as well. Joe distributed it all above the fire.

Uly helped by gathering up the plastic and paper packaging as Joe cut it open. "That's a lot of food! Is another team going to join us? I cain't wait to eat this feast."

Joe had become uncharacteristically quiet.

The men passed cold beers around and produced a folding lawn chair for each person. One of the men set out sturdy paper plates, forks, and good steak knives on the picnic table.

Since leaving that afternoon, the men hadn't stopped talking, joking, gossiping, and bragging about their families or cars or motorcycles. They went on and on about racing side-by-sides through muddy pastures at speeds that would put race-car drivers to shame. They talked shop, politics, and football.

They treated Uly like an old friend, which was amazing since they hadn't worked with him before.

Joe grilled like a pro. He didn't let it get too hot. He cooked steaks, leg quarters, and chorizos and roasted corn on the cob, peppers, and tomatoes. It smelled the way summer should and made Uly hungrier than he had been earlier.

As if on cue, the men stood up and went to the grill to load up their plates. Uly joined them and waited his turn.

"How's the beer, Uly?"

"Great, Joe. Thank you for a great day."

Joe was still being much too quiet. "Well, okay."

And that's when Joe, the grill completely empty, dropped two skimpy little burnt hot dogs on Uly's plate.

Joe smiled big. With no irony in his voice he said, "Eat up, big guy. We have a long day tomorrow!"

Uly was puzzled but still smiling. "What's this? Where's my steak?"

"Uly, the steak is expensive, and you didn't chip in. I was

worried about you, so I asked Drew to add some hot dogs to the meat order for you. These are the good ones. All beef. We didn't know what you were planning to eat. You drink our beer; you eat our food. It's not free, Uly. Everyone put their part in except you. It's a hard lesson, I know, but—"

"We don't get paid until Friday! I thought this was covered by our per diems. I don't remember hearing anything about chipping in ..."

Uly stood there in shock as the two little hot dogs rolled around on his plate, mocking him. "How was I supposed to know ..."

The other men looked away skeptically, shaking their heads. Uly was angry because this wasn't a joke. "Are you serious?"

Joe looked at Uly. "I've been waiting for you to step up and contribute like a team player. I was very clear about that in the memo. I put it in writing so there would be no miscommunication. If you don't pay attention or take responsibility, then there are consequences. You didn't do what was asked of you in the memo."

"The memo?"

"Yes. It had all the details."

"You mean the one with all the different typestyles on yellow paper? That one?"

"Yes. My memo about this trip!"

Uly's face had turned red, and his voice was louder. "Yeah, well ..."

Joe looked at him angrily, not knowing what the problem was.

Finally, Uly blurted out as he started to walk away, "Yeah? Well, I thought that was a birthday card from a clown!"

If Joe responded, Uly didn't wait around to hear it. He walked back to the hotel room still carrying his plate with its two pathetic hot dogs. He entered and slammed the door behind him. The ice-cold room smelled like industrial hospital cleaners and grapefruit juice.

Cussing, he hurled the plate of hot dogs against the wall. He went to bed hungry and angry.

RACHEL
Monday Morning

Rachel spoke to her classic car in the dark of her garage. "Good morning, Baby D."

Then she pressed a button on the wall. The garage door lifted, brightening the interior with the blue tinge of early morning light. The garage was clean and free of clutter—a place for cars, not everything else.

Rachel walked the long way around, letting the smooth surface of the car slide beneath her hand as she walked by. She promised to take Baby D to a cruise-in this week. The Doraville Diner didn't have one this Friday, but there would be one somewhere.

For now, Rachel got into her other car, a Toyota Camry. Efficient, comfortable, predictable. She sighed. She would rather drive something fun. She left for work, driving and thinking with the radio turned off.

Back when she first decided to pursue a nursing degree, her mom had warned her that nursing consisted of "long days of thankless wiping of behinds." That was unfair and turned out to be inaccurate, if not exactly wrong.

Rachel's Bachelor of Science in nursing gave her good pay and better options than many of her colleagues. Doctors or patients might occasionally find fault. Most of the time they were pleasant. She did her job without making the kinds of errors that hurt patients. If the day was long, that was the nature of work. She loved her job. It was the paperwork that was thankless.

As she had told her mom, the pay was great. The shifts were long but not insane. Since she had some seniority, she got weekends off most of the time.

Rachel left early enough to miss the peak of the morning rush hour. Some people say there is no rush-hour peak in Atlanta because it stays peaked all the time. Rachel didn't think that was exactly true, but she still expected it to be snarled up despite the early hour.

Her dad had super-practical advice about driving in Atlanta. "You have to know the route and be intentional about which lane to be in miles before you need to get into it."

She agreed and had shared his advice with friends.

Thinking about friends made her think about old friends, which got her back to thinking about Uly again. He had been gone six months with no end in sight.

He did call occasionally. He acted as if he could simply pick up where he left off weeks or a month earlier, that he could pretend they hadn't broken up, and that he could call randomly.

Did he think she wanted to talk to him, that she cared about how his day went digging holes, or that she wanted to share anything with him about how her day went?

During the last of these random calls, Rachel had blurted, "What about all the other days when you didn't call? Didn't you wonder how my day went on any of those days?"

Her outburst revealed more about how she actually felt than she had intended to reveal. Yes, she did want to share how her day went—every day. That was the problem.

They had definitely broken up but Uly, not one to complete his paperwork, had not officially broken up after all these months, even when she insisted that he acknowledge it. She, being one to complete all the paperwork in triplicate and file it appropriately, had assumed there would at least be a moment.

One day after work she and Ali had gone to Larry's Roadhouse. "You know what I mean, Ali? One last good-bye, one last opportunity to tell him how much I don't need him."

Ali had given Rachel a disapproving stare. "That's what happens with normal people."

"I know you're not a fan of Uly's."

"Did he ever buy dinner when y'all went out? Did he buy his own gas for his own car? Or was that what he dated you for?"

"Ali!"

"I know it's not any of my business but—"

"But you still judge him for what you suspect. For the record, he always paid for the meal when we went out."

"Okay. I was wrong. I'm sorry."

"Of course ..."

"What?"

Rachel had made a fist in frustration. "There is scattered chaos that surrounds Uly. And of course, he had no idea when he was leaving and of course, when he did know, he just up and left."

"Well, I know. That's what I—"

"And he's always forgetting upcoming events, always failed to return text messages, always late, always had something else going on." Rachel had stopped when she noticed the look on Ali's face. "What?"

"I just think, you know ..." Ali had trailed off without finishing.

"But he always wanted me there and included me in what he was doing and would always join me if I wanted him to come along with me. It didn't matter what it was."

For Rachel, the lack of closure was worse than breaking up. She decided that the time had long passed to stop taking his calls. She was done with the vague sense of denial that was evident in how she tended to bring him up in conversation with her friends. She was done wondering what he would think about something that happened that day. Really, it was only relevant to her. It had nothing to do with him.

My life is not relevant to him.

It was no sudden revelation. She had thought it a hundred times since he left. And it was painful.

It was rejection.

When Rachel got to work, Ali intercepted Rachel at the door to their suite of doctors' offices. "Hey, Rache! You want to get supper with us at Larry's Roadhouse after work?"

In this case the "us" was a group of work friends.

"As long as it's nobody's fake birthday."

Ali laughed. "I promise!"

Rachel shook her head. "It's not you I'm worried about."

"I know, I know! Some people need to grow up or get a hobby or something."

Rachel stopped at an unmarked door to check in with her charge nurse but stared after Ali. "I'm serious. It's ridiculous."

"Anyway"—Ali tried not to roll her eyes at Rachel—"those same people aren't working today, so I won't feel guilty when I don't invite them to join us."

"Okay, good. Talk to you later."

Silently, she considered their supper plans, *But I'm not bringing up Uly tonight! I sound pathetic when I do. I'm not even thinking about him.*

ULY
Monday Morning

"Joe's fixin' to leave, Uly! You prob'ly need to come on."

Uly's roommate had already showered, dressed, and eaten breakfast.

Uly rolled out of bed and hurried to get ready.

At the truck, the guys were not subdued by the early morning hour but were, instead, their usual jocular selves. They left Uly alone and ignored the unpleasantness of the night before.

They had all gotten up in plenty of time, made coffee, and eaten prepackaged breakfast bars or pastries in their rooms.

Uly hadn't.

His phone was dead because he hadn't charged it in the truck the day before and had forgotten to bring a charger to use in the hotel room.

Once again, he was unprepared and everyone else seemed to be on top of things.

They drove to the work site. Uly was able to charge his

phone in the truck for a few minutes.

The way it worked at the job site, one man dug a hole all the way around a pole and then moved down, leapfrogging another man who was removing soil from around the next pole down.

Joe had some tools he used to inspect the poles, including a big, gas-powered drill. For most poles, he would bore a hole below ground level and check the shavings for rot. When Joe was finished, the fourth man on their crew plugged the bore hole, treated the below-ground section of the pole to prevent rot, and wrapped it with a woven waterproofing material.

The three crewmen and Joe were constantly leapfrogging each other or, if needed, doubling back to refill the area around a pole with soil and tamp the loose soil down with a tool.

Joe took the time to document the status of each pole in detail on a rugged computer tablet before driving the truck slowly down the road to the next set of poles. They continued like that all morning.

There was a carefully orchestrated process that usually worked. Uly was used to it, but they weren't making good time this morning.

"These sand fleas are terrible!" Uly scratched his scalp. "Aren't they biting y'all? What's that spray you've got?"

"Got it at the drug store. Little spray bottle. It's expensive," one guy mumbled as he hurried by.

Soon, the sand fleas were gone since they avoided the heat

of the day. As the sun rose, the relentless heat was like that blast of hot air you get when you first open a hot oven. It must have been a hundred degrees. There was some shade, but it made no difference. Late that morning, despite having plenty of ice water in round, orange, five-gallon coolers, Uly was getting woozy from heat exhaustion and hunger.

But that wasn't why they weren't making good time.

Every hole Uly dug wasn't deep enough. No matter how wide or deep he dug it, the sand in the hole collapsed before he could get down to the required depth. Finally, Uly would get the hole deep enough but not before everyone was waiting on him.

With his tablet at his side, Joe stood there complaining. "Uly! You're going too slow."

Another hole, another complaint.

The other guys were no longer happy and joking. At lunch they wouldn't make eye contact with Uly and spent the time grumbling under their breath or laughing about things that were not obviously funny. Uly knew they weren't grumbling about the economy or telling jokes.

Uly tried to dig two more holes after lunch, but Joe didn't have any more patience. He and the other two crewmen lay into Uly with one complaint too many.

Uly stood and stretched his back. He was at least as big as the other men or bigger, but he wasn't prone to lashing out physically in anger.

He ignored the other men and looked at Joe. "You never

even asked me to help buy groceries for this trip. All you talked about was eating big and per diems. You purposefully didn't tell me a departure time this morning, or about how much hotter it would be, or about biting sand fleas."

"None of that matters, Uly. You can't even—"

"These guys are struggling with the sand too, but you act like I'm the one dragging this group down when really—"

"You are! You take twice as long to dig a hole ..."

The other guys jumped in. They didn't have to argue much longer. It was three against one. He threw his shovel, safety helmet, and orange vest on the ground, and then Uly quit his job.

He stomped away in a huff.

Then he had to turn around, pass the guys, and go to the truck to get his cell phone.

Without saying a word, he stomped away in a huff again.

He spent almost an hour walking four miles in a fast angry march back to the hotel, giving him plenty of time to rehearse what he would say on the phone to Mr. West. Uly wanted to let him know that he would be returning early and would like to be put back on his old crew. Uly didn't call him while he was walking because he was still too angry. And because he was walking fast and breathing hard, he might sound like he was crying even though he wasn't.

At the hotel, he was thankful that he had a key card to his hotel room. He took a shower, packed his bags, and then finally felt like he had calmed down enough to make the call.

"Hi, Mr. West? It's Uly."

"Uly. Talked to Joe. We'll send your last check to your home address."

"What?"

"Joe let you go twenty minutes ago."

"What?"

"Sorry, Uly. Joe is a foreman—a supervisor with authority. You can't walk away from the job and be gone two hours leaving everyone in a lurch. He let you go, and I support him."

"But I! They ... I don't have any money to get home."

"Sorry, Uly. Your last check will be mailed to you on Thursday. Not much I can do from here."

Uly had his two cheap duffel bags full of clean work clothes. He also had the pen and his cell phone but no charger. He had his wallet with his driver's license and ten bucks. There was also a handful of change that he found in one of his duffel bags.

He left the room and walked to the registration desk to ask for directions to the closest bus station.

He was desperate and realized he only had one choice.

RACHEL
Monday Afternoon

Rachel was in the middle of counting out meds for a patient with her phone on vibrate when Uly called. He had to call twice because she ignored the first call.

"Do what, Uly? I don't know what that means."

"It means—"

"I know what it means."

"But you said—"

"I mean I don't know how to wire money to you. I don't know what to think about you calling me and asking me for money. What does that mean?"

Rachel was more annoyed with herself for answering his call than she was with Uly for calling her. She was concerned about his situation, though, so she had to ask, "What's going on, Uly?"

"It's a long story and my phone battery is low. I quit my job, and I don't have any money with me."

"Quit your job!"

"Yeah."

"Where are you?"

"Savannah."

"Why did you quit your job and go to Savannah with no money?"

"I didn't."

Rachel listened to Uly inhale deeply and then exhale in a loud sigh.

He started over. "I quit my job while in Savannah on a work trip, and now I'm stranded here, so I need to buy a bus ticket to get home."

"You can catch a bus in Savannah that will take you to the middle of nowhere, south Georgia?"

"It's Albany, not 'nowhere.' But no. I quit my job, so I don't want to go back to Albany. I want to buy a ticket to Atlanta."

Rachel set her jaw and let sarcasm slip into her voice. "You have a home in Atlanta?"

He regretted using the word "home." The answer was no, he didn't. She knew he didn't have a home in Atlanta. She had one. Uly's mom had one. But Uly didn't. It didn't matter. He didn't want to stay in Albany if he didn't have a job. His job was the only reason for being there. He hardly knew anyone except his coworkers.

She regretted being sarcastic. He had always been there for her and would do anything she requested. That was true until he moved. The move had been about finding a good job, not finding a new home. She knew that.

"No. I don't actually have a home in Atlanta. I also don't have a way to get back to Albany. I mean, I just want to stay at Mom's until I can find a ride back down to my house. I'll get my truck and my stuff and move back. So, anyway ... Will you pick me up from the bus station when I get there if I call you? We can talk then. I'm sorry for bothering you at work. My phone is low—"

"Okay, okay," she interrupted, "I'll wire you—whatever that means—a hundred dollars and pick you up after you call me."

"You can probably do it from your phone with an app."

"I'll figure it out."

She quickly said good-bye and hung up on him.

ULY
Monday Afternoon

The Western Union office was several miles from the hotel at a bank downtown. He wasn't set up to receive money through an app on his phone. Even if he had been, he might lose access to the funds if he couldn't recharge the battery. He needed cash he could carry.

He grabbed his bags and looked around the hotel room to make sure he had all his belongings. Then he hoofed it over to the bank where the Western Union office was. It wasn't hard to find with a quick search in a map app. He then turned off his phone.

Rachel had figured it out, and he was able to receive the hundred dollars she sent him.

He was grateful. He had never asked her for money. It was a point of pride that he paid for their dates, although she would always insist on paying if they met for lunch. He never asked anyone for money, except his mom in the past before he had a real job, but not recently.

Now that it was done, he considered what his options might have been. It would have been humiliating to ask for money from anyone he worked with back in Albany. He didn't have anyone else there to ask, so it hadn't been a real possibility.

Then, of course, he could have called his mom or grandmother. They wouldn't have been able to figure out how to wire money to him, so that hadn't been a good choice either.

Old friends back home weren't the people he wanted to be explaining all of this to. Not that any of them had any money.

It was about Rachel. He had already decided that. To him it was about rebuilding a relationship with her. But he knew what her friends would say. He wasn't sure they were wrong.

He realized he had forgotten something important. He turned the phone back on and texted her a quick thank you.

Next, he left the bank and went to look for the bus station the bank teller told him about. It had once been a Greyhound station, but it wasn't anymore. The building was old but not faded and worn out. In fact, this place had been expertly restored to historic art-deco perfection.

And it was a fancy restaurant.

Confused, he stepped in and asked about the bus station. The nice lady behind a podium at the door pointed him in the right direction. He then left the restaurant and continued walking east down MLK, Jr. Boulevard, which was exactly the wrong direction, until he came to a corner lot that had once been a gas station and convenience store. It was now a bus station. The new, backlit sign read "East Coast Metro Lines."

Not Greyhound anymore, I guess, since that's a restaurant now.

The waiting area was clean and new. He walked through it to the ticket counter and bought a fifty-nine-dollar ticket for a one-way trip to Atlanta.

A queue had already formed under an awning outside the ticketing office. It was made up of people who looked like they were in the same boat as him: cheap luggage, heat exhausted, on foot, old clothes, duct-taped shoes, or dollar-store flip-flops. Some looked like they had slept on the street. A few were old before their time. There was also a young mother with a crying infant and a grandmother.

An old bus that had been new in 1960 rolled up with brakes screeching and the diesel engine knocking. The bus's lower third was well-blackened by road grime, and it rocked to a squeaking halt at the bus stop.

The old doors opened with a sudden crash. The driver was ancient and spindly and wore huge, black sunglasses. Loose skin hanging from his bald head twisted around his neck. As he looked at the line of passengers, his head swiveled on his shoulders instead of merely turning. Uly expected him to flip a sticky tongue out to catch a fly.

The driver stared at him.

Riders got off the bus, banging open the old doors on the luggage hold.

In utter shock, Uly watched as little kids tumbled out to join their anxious parents who had been regular passengers on the bus.

"Kids rode in the luggage hold!" Uly exclaimed aloud to the people in the line. They never made eye contact with him and didn't acknowledge what happened.

Uly left the line and ran behind the bus to see where the kids and their families had gone, but they had disappeared into the crowd or jumped into waiting cars or something.

All the adults and children were gone except for one grandmother who was walking purposefully toward a car holding a child's hand. She was fumbling with an oversized pocketbook in her other hand. A compact umbrella was tucked against her side with her elbow. While poking around for her keys, she dropped the umbrella on the road and continued to her car without noticing it had fallen.

Uly ran to the umbrella to give it back to her, but by the time he picked it up and looked around she was gone. Mind reeling, he turned around, looking for the kids and their families. It seemed unbelievable that there had been stowaways on the bus.

He stumbled back to the line of people getting on the bus and saw the unsmiling lizard-man bus driver taking tickets as passengers boarded. Right then and there, fear gripped him so badly he walked away.

There was no way he was getting on that bus.

After a while, Uly calmed down and decided that before

exchanging his unused ticket for a new one, he would go across the street to a convenience store to buy some snacks for his trip.

After shopping around for a few minutes, he spent twelve dollars and stocked up with two twenty-ounce Cokes, a bag of potato chips, four Snickers bars, and a big bag of beef jerky. That would tide him over until he could get back to Atlanta. He would be hungry by the time he got home the next morning, but then he would get breakfast and be good to go.

He stored some food in each duffel bag along with the umbrella the grandmother had dropped, and then he walked back to the ticket counter at the bus station. A nicely designed colorful sign exclaimed that East Coast Metro Lines was happy to exchange tickets.

He walked back to the ticket counter and offered the ticket to the young clerk. "Hi. I missed the bus to Atlanta. Can I exchange this ticket for a later bus?"

The clerk's poufy hair bounced as she spoke. "Sure, hun. Be right with you."

She had a pleasant, singsong, Southern drawl. "You still goin' to A'lan'a?"

Uly nodded. "Yes, ma'am."

She smiled and looked at Uly. "Okay, that'll be fifty-nine dollars."

"What? I already paid that much for the first ticket and that was only twenty minutes ago! What kind of stupid—"

Her gaze snapped up at him while she waited for him to

continue, but he caught himself before digging that hole any deeper. Then Uly decided she was already offended by whatever it was he had not actually said.

She stared at him, enunciating each word—even "Atlanta"—precisely, all pretense of saccharine sweetness gone. "And your second one will be fifty-nine more for a whole new ticket since there aren't any more buses leaving for Atlanta today. Exchanges are only good for the day of."

She paused. "However—"

"But—" Uly stopped himself before interrupting her any further.

The attitude softened some. "I'm working with you here, sir, because I know ..." The attitude didn't soften much. She looked at Uly and continued her thought, giving him a thin smile. "... you had to make a special run to get that all-important bag of Fritos and then you got yourself bus-left."

"Well, I don't have fifty-nine bucks for a whole new ticket."

"Just bear with me while I look into it, sir."

Her attitude reminded Uly of the two mocking little hot dogs rolling around on his plate the night before.

She started to speak again. "Okay, hun ..." Then she paused while looking at a computer screen, perplexed. "Hmm." Finally, pleasant again. "It looks like I can get you on the late bus for the price of an exchange. That's only twenty-four dollars. It doesn't technically get you there today, but it is the next bus to A'lan'a, so I can waive the exchange policy."

Uly was confused but didn't want to question her.

Then she was back to her severe attitude. "Okay, sir. Your bus leaves, as in departs, pulls out of the station, at exactly 5:10 p.m. Um-kay?"

Uly paid the additional twenty-four dollars and waited hours.

He paced, drank both Cokes, and was wired. He waited on the hard benches.

After three hours, a bus pulled into the loading area.

Uly watched the slow crawl of Georgia cities across the digital destination sign. "—Atlanta—Macon—Savannah—"

The bus had been built sometime this century. Good. He checked the luggage hold. No stowaways. Good. He had food and luggage. Good. He was finally going home.

Uly found a seat against a window, settled in, and waited. The idling engine hadn't stopped, and eventually the well-groomed, smartly dressed bus driver, wearing a company tie, smoothly pulled the bus out of the station on time.

He was on his way back to where he should have been all along. His seat was comfortable, and he enjoyed the restful break at the end of a long, weird day.

After almost two hours, something about the change in road or engine noise or people moving around awakened Uly from a nap. As the bus went around a long curve, he looked to the right out the big window beside him. In the distance, he saw the tall towers of a long, cable-stayed bridge crossing a wide river.

And that was completely wrong.

Nothing like that exists anywhere in Macon or Atlanta, Georgia.

A cold knot formed in Uly's stomach.

The coach exited the interstate and made several turns before arriving at the East Coast Metro Lines bus station a few minutes later. Uly stepped off, looking for any sign that would tell him where he had landed. He looked at the digital sign on the front of the bus still scrolling the cities. "—Atlanta—Macon—Savannah—Charleston—Columbia—Greenville—Knoxville—"

He stood there, unmoving, and watched the list scroll by again. "Chattanooga—Atlanta—Macon—Savannah—Charleston—"

He was in Charleston!

He immediately and irrationally hated Charleston.

He again thought of those mocking hot dogs rolling around on his plate. He thought about the men complaining about him not being able to dig holes. He thought about the sand fleas and Mr. West telling him he was fired. He thought of the lizard-man bus driver. Then there was the poufy-haired clerk at the bus station who was either incompetent or vindictive. He didn't know which.

He also considered how big a mess he was in. He needed to travel west three-hundred miles to get to Atlanta.

The sky was bright, but the sun had dipped well below the tops of nearby trees and would set in the next thirty minutes or so. But because it was summer and the skies were clear, it would be light enough to see for another hour or more. He munched on beef jerky and looked around.

East Coast Metro Lines had renovated a corner gas station for their Charleston stop. It looked like it had once been a large property that could serve semitrucks. Much larger truck stops were more common now, so this gas station must have lost out to bigger facilities closer to the interstate before East Coast Metro Lines turned it into a bus stop.

He walked to the corner of the crossroads and turned back to look at the bus station. He could see the big bridge from here. The river, the bridge, and the Atlantic Ocean were in that direction.

Don't go that way.

He pivoted on the balls of his feet and faced the setting sun. He had no plan and no idea how to get back to Savannah, much less Atlanta. At least he was facing the right direction.

ULY
Monday Evening

Across the road from where Uly was standing at the crossroads, a row of old homes faced east. Most of them were craftsman-style homes with long front porches and square, tapered wooden columns resting on stone pillars. One immediately across the road from him was a Victorian with wrap-around porches and round corner towers sporting conical roofs. It was painted white with black doors and shutters. The craftsman houses were a variety of muted colors. Many of them had neat little wooden signs out front indicating they were used for one business or another. One had the words "interior designs" and another one had an artsy edge to it with a sign that said something about candles.

A tall, slim, elderly woman appeared around the corner of the imposing Victorian home across the road. A sign out front read "The MacAllister Victorian" in bronze lettering and under that "A Bed & Breakfast, Est. 1950."

Using a rollator, the old lady walked with a shuffling gait

through a manicured front lawn to a sidewalk extending from the steps to the street.

Once on the sidewalk, she turned away from the street. Then, leaving the rollator behind, she grasped a handrail on the steps leading to the front porch. She began a doddering climb, taking each step with great deliberation.

Uly couldn't simply watch her. What if she fell while he did nothing? He checked for cars and then crossed the street.

He approached the house. "Hello. Ma'am? Hello!"

The woman's steady upward progress ground to a halt. She carefully rotated, swapped hands on the handrail, and then made a glacial, shuffling turn. She looked in Uly's direction but still didn't acknowledge him.

Finally, licking her lips and adjusting her dentures, she made eye contact with him. "What." It wasn't a question.

"Um ... can I help you?"

"Are you the idiot who left a delivery on my front porch?"

"Um ... no."

"Then, yes. You can help me young man."

Uly paused a second, trying to process the situation. Why hadn't she opened the front door to get the package? Would she have refused his help if he had been "the idiot who left a delivery" on her front porch?

She had already turned back to her task with renewed vigor. "Or you can just stand there."

"No. I, um, I can get that for you."

Uly ran up the steps, picked up the box, and turned to take

it back down the steps to the old lady.

She had turned and was making her way back to her walker.

Uly waited on the sidewalk while she steadied herself using the rollator's handlebars. She pulled a light sweater out of a basket on the front of the walker and hung it over her arm. "You can put that right there." She pointed at the basket twice.

Uly gently placed the box into the basket and took a step back.

She popped a lever to release the brake. "Thank you, young man."

"You're welcome. Um, I'm Uly."

She studied him, scowling, and sucked on a tooth with a disapproving click. "I'm Lucy MacAllister."

She spun around surprisingly fast and headed back the way she had come in that same slow shuffle, then said, "Come on, Biscuit, let's get you some supper."

Uly followed her and wondered why she called him "Biscuit."

At that moment, a teacup Yorkie zipped by his feet and dashed ahead of Lucy.

She stopped and turned, smiling for the first time. "Come on, Uly." She turned back, continuing her slow journey. "We'll get you some supper, too."

Uly followed Lucy to the top of the ramp onto a side porch and through a door into a small commercial kitchen with gleaming stainless steel counter tops and heavy appliances with large knobs. Everything was spotlessly clean but at least thirty years old.

Inside the house, Lucy was much more confident of her footing, so she put the rollator aside. She heated up beef stew in a brass pot on the stove, talking to Uly the whole time. "If I fall, I'm done, so I have to be careful outside."

When the stew was hot, she pointed to a plate full of large biscuits. Uly knew they were handmade because each one had three indentions on top that were made when Lucy patted them out. "I made those this morning. Get as many as you want. My husband used to bust them open and ladle stew over them. Eat it with a fork."

Uly thought that sounded perfect.

Lucy invited Uly to follow her across a wide hallway to the dining room. She set his place at the table and then left Uly to eat alone. The food was wonderful but eating in the formal dining room by himself reminded him that he was truly alone in life.

He looked around. The walls were full of old paintings and photos of men and women with severe expressions. Heavy drapes on the windows imposed a quietness on the room. Glass doors beneath the marble top of a sideboard revealed crystal goblets in the cabinets.

After he had finished eating, he crossed the wide hallway back into the kitchen.

"Just put your dishes in the sink."

"Thank you, Mrs. Lucy. I appreciate the hospitality, but I should—"

"No. You're a guest here tonight."

"Well, I need to save my money for a bus ticket, so I can—"

"No. I have an empty house with ten bedrooms, and you need a place to sleep. The third-floor guest suite will be perfect for you. The bathroom is clean and stocked with linens. There's a nice place to sit and read in the front tower with a view of the bridge. I have a girl who comes in and does the cleaning."

Uly wasn't turning down a place to sleep. "Okay."

She waited.

He looked at her and it dawned on him why she was waiting. "Yes. Thank you!"

While washing dishes, she returned to a conversation they had earlier. "So, you said you quit your job?"

"Yes ma'am. I walked off the job today. I'm not going back even if they beg."

"Because your boss was mean to you?"

"Well. I wouldn't say it that way. He wasn't—"

"People are so quick to take offense these days."

"Right. That was part of it. He didn't like—"

"No. I meant you. You were too quick to take offense."

Uly was offended by that remark. "Well, um, it just wasn't going to work."

"But it's none of my business, now, is it, Uly? Come on. Follow me to the den."

Uly followed, surprised he wasn't still defending himself.

Lucy walked out of the kitchen and stopped in the wide hallway running from the front to the back of the house. It split the first floor into two main sections.

She pointed to a door on her left. "Back door. We don't use it."

Uly looked out the wavy glass to a porch nestled into the back corner of the house. There was another exterior door onto the porch farther down. He turned to follow Lucy. The coffered ceiling was covered in heart-pine squares, each one trimmed with complicated molding and inset with heart-pine panels made of tongue-and-groove bead board.

She stopped with her hand on a wide terminal baluster at the base of the heart-pine stairs. It was topped by a bronze statue of a woman wearing a dress with folds cascading to her feet. She had slender arms and her hands were held out in a welcoming gesture. The statue stood under a bouquet of roses with bronze stems and white glass petals. Lucy toggled a hidden button, turning on small lamps inside the roses. "I'll leave this lamp on during the night in case you need to come downstairs."

Lucy continued down the broad hallway, stopping before reaching the front door. Fourteen-foot-tall double-pocket doors with ornate carved panels spanned six-foot-wide openings on either side of the foyer near the front door.

She turned to her left to face the closed double doors there. When she pulled one pocket door open, hidden pulleys opened its matching door, revealing an ornately decorated room full of wingback chairs and two formal sofas. The room had four curio cabinets with glass doors protecting dainty ceramic figurines. Louis XIV coffee tables with curvy legs were placed in front of the sofas. "This is the parlor."

She crossed the hall to the other set of double doors and opened them. "This is the den."

A massive painting of antebellum Charleston harbor hung above the mantle. Ornate frames surrounding large, rectangular paintings of men wearing uniforms covered the walls. Black-and-white photos in oval frames hung around the paintings. Leather chairs with wide round arms sat against the walls near the door and in the cove made by a tower on the corner of the house.

"I should leave these doors open. Helps with the airflow in the house."

Then she continued down the hall to the wide double doors at the front of the house. She made a show of trying to open them without success. "That package you retrieved for me—I've been waiting for it for a week. The UPS man and the mailman and that FedEx boy know they're supposed to take their deliveries around to the table at the top of the wheel-chair ramp"—she pulled unsuccessfully on the front door again—"because this door swells from the humidity in the summer and I'm not strong enough to open it. And then, if I do, I can't close it, so I don't use it at all."

"I could fix it."

"No. I don't want it fixed. I want my deliveries to come to the kitchen door. If you fix it so it works now it won't close properly in the winter."

She went back to the den and pointed to two matching wingback chairs sitting at angles in front of the inert, soot-blackened fireplace. Tall, narrow windows in the room were framed by heavy curtains. Beneath all the framed portraits, slightly textured and uneven plaster painted a warm white stopped at ornate heart-pine panels that trimmed the lower third of the walls. The room was well lit and bright despite the heavy curtains and dark wood trim.

"I'm telling you all that so you don't get into your head that you're going to surprise me with the 'wonderful favor' of fixing my door."

She carefully sat down in one chair, and Uly joined her in the other. "Oh, okay. Yes, ma'am."

Biscuit appeared and leapt into her lap, all jittery and frantic, but he calmed down immediately once she scratched his ears. "So, this afternoon, I put my sweater on to take Biscuit to potty. I was standing on the side porch there at the top of the wheelchair ramp when I saw you step off that bus looking like you didn't know which way was up. Most people have somebody waiting, or they go to a car, or something."

Uly was nodding and listening. "Right. I didn't—"

"But you walked in circles like you didn't know where you were. Then I got to the bottom of the ramp, and that's when I saw that package sitting up there at the front door."

Uly was awestruck by the house. He estimated it had six-teen-foot-high ceilings—double the height of most modern homes. It was immaculate and ornate. On the long mantle above the fireplace and hearth, there was a large collection of framed photos of all kinds: new, color, old, and black and white. They were all different sizes in different frames.

To one side, partially hidden by a framed photo, a roy-al-blue marble bigger than a golf ball sat on a heavy-looking brass ring.

Uly absently scratched his head where the sand-flea bites were making it itch.

Lucy continued her story. "So, I took my sweater off be-cause it's too blamed hot in the middle of summer for a sweat-er. I was so mad I decided I was going to get my package right then and there."

Uly had gotten up and was standing in front of the fire-place. He took his time looking at the unusual marble.

"But you came along at precisely the right time."

She paused when he didn't respond. "My antique marble. It originally belonged to Roanoke's great-grandfather. We thought it fit the house. It's a conversation starter."

Uly reached up and ventured to touch it. "I've never seen anything like it."

"Yes. It is quite unusual. There's some long yarn about it that Roanoke used to read to guests on rainy days. He picked up the story from his father when he was a little boy. I used to have the marble on display all by itself, but my pictures mean

more to me now. We don't get as many guests as we once did."
She said "we" like Roanoke was still alive. "I don't need to
have as many conversation starters sitting around."

"Mrs. Lucy, this whole house is one big conversation
starter."

"You are right about that, young man."

Uly continued to peer at the glass ball, mesmerized by the
way light seemed to well up out of its interior. "You still have
guests?"

"Old friends. Or the elderly children of old friends." She
laughed at the irony of the words. "We still book a night or
two every month. I have a girl who comes in to do the cleaning upstairs. I still do most of the cooking. Me and Sister
Schubert."

Uly turned around smiling. "Good rolls."

She nodded with a conspiratorial twinkle in her eye. "The
old folks think I still make those yeast rolls by hand, so don't
tell 'em."

She continued telling him about the house. "A landscape
company takes care of the yard. I suppose I put the electri-
cian's kids through college. This old place ..." She trailed off,
looking around and shaking her head. "Roanoke did most everything as long as he could. He passed ten years ago."

Uly sat back down, watching Lucy. She was lost in thought.
He waited until she stirred again. She turned to him with a
gentle smile he had not yet seen.

Then it was gone.

"I have bridge club at ten o'clock in the morning. Breakfast is at eight. Don't be late. You'll need to be on your way back to Georgia. There are buses leaving all day going that way, so you'll be fine. Don't worry about making your bed. I have a girl who comes in to do the cleaning."

Uly stood, not wanting to admit he was almost out of money and not wanting to beg. "Well. I mean, I guess I'll see if I can get a bus ticket back to Georgia in the morning. Thank you for giving me a place to stay."

Lucy nodded. "The third-floor suite is all the way to the top of the stairs and directly above us here at the front of the house. Good night, Uly."

Uly told Lucy good night and went upstairs to find his room. After a shower, Uly relaxed in a wingback chair next to a small round side table. The chair and the table were in the circular area in the corner of his room in the tower that extended from the ground through all three floors. The windows in the tower provided a panoramic view of Charleston with the brightly lit cable-stayed bridge in the distance dominating the view.

Uly wondered how much it cost to stay at The MacAllister Victorian if you were a paying guest. He had never been in a hotel room as nice as this one.

A book was on the side table. It was made of standard-sized copier paper bound with a plastic binding that curved through dozens of little square holes punched into the left margin of the paper.

"The Glassblower's Apprentice" was typewritten on the card stock cover. He opened it. The book's photocopied pages full of old-fashioned typewriter text had yellowed with age.

Flipping randomly to the middle of the book, Uly began to read, but he fell asleep sitting up in the chair before he needed to turn the page.

RACHEL
Tuesday Morning

Rachel slept well all night in the comfort of her own home. She had no intention of letting worry for Uly ruin anything: sleep, life, work, or friendships.

She had said a prayer for him the night before, as she did every day, and then she had gone to bed.

Now, in the early morning darkness, she finished her coffee expecting a text or phone call or something, but Uly hadn't tried to get in touch yet, which was fine. It was still early.

She had no idea when he would arrive at the bus station. He would call when he did, and then he could wait until she could get there. And that would be a long day because she was about to go to work for a twelve-hour shift that started at seven a.m.

And I'm certainly not mentioning this to Ali.

Her colleagues at work, her informal supper club, would not be patient with her if they knew she was expecting a call from Uly. They would be scornful if they knew he had borrowed money, and especially if they knew he might be back in her life.

Not that he was back in her life.

He's not back in my life, Ali!

She caught herself practicing defending her decision to answer his call. Then she was annoyed with herself while also being annoyed with Uly.

People are going to be able to tell I'm annoyed.

She wanted to be in a pleasant mood when she got to work. To fight the annoyance, she hurried to finish getting ready. She brushed her hair and applied lip gloss. Then she grabbed her purse, checked it for her keys and phone, and went to the garage. She turned on the lights and greeted her Baby D.

She opened the door and got in. It had been restored so it shut with a satisfying thunk. She breathed in the smell of the new, oiled leather upholstery covering the interior of the car while admiring a dashed line of perfect white stitching.

Rachel put her hands on the steering wheel. She had completely forgotten about Uly.

Almost.

LUCY
Tuesday Morning

At ninety-four, Lucy didn't get up at the crack of dawn; she often slept late. It was already six-thirty and the sun was up when she climbed out of bed to get ready for the day.

The MacAllister Victorian was originally built in the 1890s. To reduce the risk of burning the house down, the kitchen had been built as a separate building behind the main house. Cooked food was carried from the kitchen to the keeping room in the outrigger, a projection off the back of the house. The formal dining room had been accessed through the butler's pantry which was between the keeping room and the dining room. There had been another pantry in this section of the house for dry goods storage. A corridor to a back staircase gave access to a separate suite of rooms upstairs for cooks and other employees who lived in the house.

After World War One, the keeping room and pantries had been turned into living space for the family that lived in the house. Then, during the Great Depression, the house had been used for boarding itinerant farm workers.

When Lucy and Roanoke bought it, they remodeled the floor plan of the projecting outrigger space to create an apartment for themselves. Lucy still used their apartment as her private residence.

Biscuit stretched in his dog bed and waited for Lucy to finish getting ready for the day. Then they went together to the kitchen to get breakfast.

Lucy made coffee, cooked crispy French toast with cinnamon and sugar, link sausages—two for Uly, one for herself—and a shallow serving bowl of scrambled eggs. She opened the door to let Biscuit go outside on his own recognizance and then sat at a small table in the kitchen to eat her breakfast.

A few minutes before eight o'clock, while she was setting his place, Uly walked into the dining room dressed in a T-shirt, blue jeans, and his work boots. "Morning."

Lucy poured coffee into a delicate coffee cup for him. "Good morning, Uly. Enjoy. You know the drill."

She disappeared back across the central hallway to the kitchen where she prepared hors d'oeuvres to take to the bridge club meeting.

Uly ate quickly and then went to the kitchen with his dishes. "Thank you, Uly. Bringing those in here saves me some steps. At my age I have to save them up to use later."

"Thank you for everything, Mrs. Lucy."

"You're welcome."

"So did you open this place in 1892?"

"No. That's when I built it."

Uly laughed at her quick comeback.

"Roanoke and I bought this house after the war. It had been mistreated; chopped up into apartments. We lived here and spent three years renovating it to turn it into an inn. We didn't open until 1950. It was tough. But we were young and happy."

"That actually sounds very cool."

Lucy was all business, washing and putting away the dishes as she talked. "I've been running this place ever since. We were so young." She shook her head, thinking. Then she continued. "We tore out all the electrical and plumbing and redid it in the '90s. I've lost count of the number of times the bathrooms have had to be renovated."

"How do you keep going—stay healthy and active after all these years?"

While drying her hands, Lucy answered in a matter-of-fact tone without thinking about it. "Trust in the Lord."

Uly stood there not responding, surprised by her answer.

She opened the exterior kitchen door to let Biscuit back inside. "Alright. Get your luggage. Doris will be here in a minute to pick me up to go play bridge, and I'm locking up the store for the day."

"Okay. My bags are in the den."

Lucy put her sweater on while Uly went to get his duffel bags. "You sure you don't want me to fix that front door?" he asked when he walked back into the kitchen.

She gave him a withering look while holding the door to the side porch open. "Go back to Georgia, Uly."

She held her hand out for him to shake.

He shook it gently. "So long, Mrs. Lucy."

ULY
Tuesday Morning

Uly walked across the lush lawn and stopped at the busy street in front of the MacAllister Victorian.

A bus entered the bus station as another one departed.

Trust in the Lord.

Uly crossed the street and walked into the bus station. He stood looking at a chart on a wall in the ticketing area but didn't want to enter the line because he only had fifteen dollars and some change. The cheapest bus to Savannah and on to Atlanta was thirty-four dollars. Uly turned and exited the building. He didn't want to beg for money from strangers.

He called Rachel. He hated the thought of begging her for money again but didn't get the chance. There was no answer. She was at work. Her phone wouldn't let him leave a voicemail.

Uly started walking north on the opposite side of the street from Mrs. Lucy's. Most of the houses didn't look residential. Instead, as he had noticed the day before, they seemed to be occupied by businesses.

When he was well past the law firms and CPAs, he found an old church and some houses which had been turned into restaurants and the kinds of places tourists would want to visit like clothing stores, an old bookstore, souvenir shops, and a fudge shop.

One of these was a rambling old house painted sky blue with an array of used bicycles parked out front. Colorful pennants were strung around the big wraparound porch. Tourists and young people in their twenties were milling around, coming and going with cones of ice cream. Music from inside the store drifted down the street.

A bicycle would get him back to Savannah.

He thought of Lucy drying her hands on a towel and saying in the most casual way, "Trust in the Lord."

A man was walking in front of Uly. He had sun-and-saltwater bleached blond hair that looked like it had only ever been brushed with his fingers. He was wearing board shorts, flip-flops, and a faded old tank top with graphics on the back that said something about Folly Beach on it above a bunch of logos. He was tanned extremely dark and looked like he never did anything but surf.

Uly followed him to the front porch. A sign above the steps read "Dippy's Nibbles-the-Cat Thrift & Surf Ice-Cream Parlor." A logo of an angry cat chewing a surfboard dominated the sign.

When the man walked into the store, a number of workers and customers greeted him.

"Dip! Dip! Dip!"

"Dee-yup!"

"Dippy-Dippy-Dipster."

"Nibbles-the-Cat's in the house!"

"He's back!"

"He's not Nibbles, that's what Nibbles dragged in!"

"I guess we have to go back to acting like we're working."

Uly watched as they greeted the owner of the store. Several people gave him big hugs.

He stopped and turned, flashing a perfect smile in all directions. "Y'all are too much. I've only been gone a week."

Inside the store, most of the walls had been removed. The ceiling had also been removed and the rafters were visible. Load-bearing poles held up the roof. To Uly's right, small tables with chairs were crowded near a long counter with ice-cream coolers. High on the wall behind the coolers, the cat logo looked out over the store with a sign reading, "Dippy's Nibbles-the-Cat Ice-Cream Parlor."

A young man stood behind the counter taking orders from people standing in a short line. He packed cones full and quickly served each customer huge softball-sized double-stacked scoops of ice cream on waffle cones.

To Uly's left and at the back of the building were more signs with Nibbles-the-Cat logos for different sections of the store. There was a surf shop at the back and a thrift store at the front.

Customers continued to greet Dippy and ask him how he

was doing. "Where have you been, Dip? Were you sick?"

He seemed to know everyone, although Uly thought that was more about his personality than his actual relationships with the people there. "I'm fine. My mother-in-law was in a car accident. My wife and her sister left town to go see about her. I *chaphromed* our kids and the cousins all week. I knew my crew had things under control here."

One of the store employees standing with him explained to the crowd of surfers and thrift store regulars, "Yeah, that was, what, last Wednesday?"

"Yeah. She was in a *corner* for a while."

Customers nodded, listening and empathizing. "Oh my goodness."

A few more people joined the crowd around Dippy. "She had to have emergency surgery on a cracked *reverberator* in her neck or she would've been paralyzed."

Uly scrunched up his face and looked at Dippy.

Her what?

No one else seemed to be confused by his story.

Dippy nodded with a grave look on his face. "Complicated by the fact that she was on a *resurrection* machine the whole time. But the machine did its job. She woke up and the docs say she should fully recover."

Uly walked away avoiding the crowd and thinking: *corner, cracked reverberators, resurrection machine? This guy must be cracked in his reverberators, whatever those are!*

The crowd was dispersing. Dippy moved toward the ice-cream counter and some of his friends followed. "Y'all want some *corn* ice cream? *Napoleon* is my favorite."

One old guy was all in. "Yeah! You buying?"

Dippy encouraged everyone. "Get in line."

Uly was sure he didn't want any corn ice cream—*what is Napoleon ice cream?*

An employee of the store approached Uly with a friendly smile. "Can I help you, sir?"

"Um, yeah." Uly was still trying to listen to Dippy talking to customers at the ice-cream counter. Was he saying words incorrectly or was Uly hearing them wrong? He wasn't sure. The employee looked at him, waiting patiently.

Uly refocused on her. "I was wondering about buying one of the bicycles outside."

"Okay. We have the best thrift-store prices on bikes anywhere. Price tags are on them. The surf shop will adjust the seat if you need them to. Go ahead and pick out the one you want."

"Okay. Thanks."

The cheapest one was twelve dollars and too big for most people. It was a heavy old ten-speed with a rack behind the seat. Uly thought it would be perfect. He test drove it and then went in to pay. Dippy was still holding court in the ice-cream shop. Uly decided the seat would work the way it was.

He walked to the sidewalk, pushing his new bike. He looked back at the store with the logo of the cat biting a surfboard and wondered what Lucy MacAllister thought of Dippy the surf-shop guy?

Traffic wasn't too bad. Using his belt he strapped both of his duffel bags to the rear rack. Then he jumped on the bike and pointed it south. A bus in the distance was headed the way he wanted to go, so he followed it until it got out of sight. A while later another bus passed him, and he followed it. This was the way home.

Trust in the Lord.

After an hour of riding, the highway became a four-lane with a wide, paved shoulder. Riding was easy, and it gave him time to think.

He was hungry. He stopped at a gas station and bought a cheap ham sandwich. It tasted like cardboard, but it was something. He got back on the bike and continued down the road.

He had hated Charleston when he stepped off that bus the day before, but now he was glad he had made this minor detour. It wouldn't be too long before he could get back to the bus stop in Savannah, talk to Rachel, buy a ticket, and get back to Atlanta.

Uly's bike was heavy, but it was in good condition and served him well while he bicycled for many miles. He hadn't ridden a bike in a long time. He enjoyed pedaling hard up the slight rises and the feeling of speed as he tore back down the hill. The four-lane highway wasn't very busy, and the cars that did go by typically moved over to keep from getting too close to him.

Then his front tire rolled over a piece of curved metal on

the shoulder of the road that instantly flipped into the front wheel's spokes. Half the spokes broke when the metal lodged against the front forks. The wheel collapsed with a terrible clanging noise. The handlebars snatched out of his hands and the wheel forks dug into the pavement, stopping the bike. Uly went from riding along peacefully to being launched onto the pavement. He skidded and tumbled, getting road rash up and down his bare arms and on his right leg despite the protection the jeans provided.

He sat up, groaning and bleeding from several pulpy, round wounds and a few more long scrapes. He was in terrible pain and he was shaking, taking deep, ragged breaths.

After a minute or two, he calmed down. He checked his wounds and felt his head, trying to determine if he was bleeding from any areas he couldn't see. For several minutes he plucked bits of gravel from the wounds and remembered the time he had been airborne on the go-kart. It had been a hard landing, but at least it had been into water.

He stood up and looked at the bike. It was ruined. The front tire was in the shape of a heart, the front forks were badly bent, and the handlebars were skewed sideways.

He looked down the road and blew a big sigh. This didn't change anything.

He unstrapped his duffel bags and shoved the bike off the pavement. Then he continued walking in the direction he had been going for the last several hours.

MARTI
Tuesday Evening

In the choir loft of the host church in Charleston following the choir's last performance for the revival, Marti was gathering up a few remaining items and putting them in a black milk crate. She could hear some of the choir members talking at an exit door behind the choir loft.

"Bill?" someone hollered from the back parking lot. She was sure it was Tye. Bill was standing at the door.

"Hey, Bill. The trailer is hitched up, and I checked the brake lights for you."

"Okay, thanks. Alright, the equipment is all here. I'm going back into the sanctuary to look around and see if Marti needs help with anything."

Tye followed Bill into the cool quiet of the sanctuary.

A few members of the church were straightening up following the end of the service as a group of chatting people moved toward the front doors. Lights were already off in the main sanctuary.

A young man walked by Marti to cut off the lights in the choir loft. "It sure was good having y'all here this week, Marti."

"Oh, thank you, Pastor. This has been delightful!"

Bill and Tye stepped up into the choir loft to help Marti.

"Some people like to disappear when there's work to do," grumped Tye.

Marti wished he wouldn't say things like that around their host.

Tye shook his head, looking at Marti. "I hope we're going to have more help loading the trailer than just us."

Marti picked up her milk crate. "They'll be here. They just had to get their luggage."

She could have been grumpy that Tye was grumpy. However, Tye was probably proud he had been so tactful. There had been a time when he was much harsher.

Bill held the back door open for Tye as he carried an equipment box out, followed by Marti with her crate. Then Bill picked up a box and carried it out.

A new Chevy Tahoe pulled up next to the group's equipment trailer.

The driver lowered his side window as he stopped. "Sorry we're late getting y'all on the road." Several members of the traveling music ministry got out of the SUV and pulled luggage out of the back of the vehicle.

Bill stopped at the driver's window briefly. "It's okay. It won't take but a minute for us to load up."

A lady in the passenger seat leaned forward to speak to

Marti, who joined Bill. "We're returning the soprano section to you, Marti. We sure did enjoy having y'all."

"Honey, you're so welcome. Let me tell you, we are so glad we were able to be here."

Some people thought she came across as fake, even sarcastic, but she was naturally expressive.

Another car pulled up and some more choir members exited it as a few more appeared from around a corner, pulling rolling luggage.

One of the choir members came around from behind the SUV and thanked the driver and his wife. "We enjoyed staying at your beautiful home."

Others chimed in with more thanks.

The twelve members of the music ministry had broken into groups and stayed in church members' homes on Sunday and Monday night after singing at the church's revival and camp meeting. The church's regular choir and lead singer would be leading music on the final day's revival service tomorrow.

The host families helped the choir members unload their luggage from the cars. A few others drove around to the back of the church so the choir members wouldn't have to drag their luggage all over the church grounds.

A few more church members showed up, and they loaded the sound equipment and luggage in less than ten minutes. They said their good-byes with handshakes and hugs all around.

"Thank you, Marti! See y'all next year!"

"What's for supper?" someone in the back of the van asked before they had pulled out of the parking lot.

Bill was driving, but that didn't make him in charge of anything. He was just the member who was most willing to drive while towing a trailer. He was definitely not going to pick a place, recommend a place, or even veto the group's choice.

Marti sometimes acted like she was in charge of more than music, but not everyone cared to follow her lead unless she was actually directing music. Sometimes not even then.

"Maybe something quick everyone can agree on," she began hopefully, trying to open negotiations to set a direction and tone that would not lead to a stalemate or war or, worse yet, cold war.

Their disagreements were not bad as long as they weren't trying to agree on a place to eat. Her opening tactic had started some conversations in the back of the van.

"No Italian."

"I wish we could all sit together."

"I hope there's something other than fast food."

"I can't stand the smell of fish."

"How long before we eat?"

These were a few of the comments she heard. She knew who had said them too.

Marti, riding shotgun, looked at Bill. They had been doing this long enough to know what to do.

With enough projection to be heard at the back of the van,

Bill said, "I have to stop to get gas before we get too far down the road, so we can stop and eat in less than an hour."

Marti chimed in on cue for the whole van to hear, "We'll pull in somewhere with a number of options. We don't all have to eat at the same place."

When they finally stopped, the gas station was surrounded by restaurants with enough variety among the ones still open to accommodate differing appetites.

As everyone piled out of the van, Marti gave some direction. "About thirty minutes, y'all. We need to get back on the road as soon as we can."

After filling the van with gas, Bill pulled to the outer edge of the large paved parking area to get out of the way of other motorists. Then he, Marti, and a few other members of the choir walked over to a burger place to eat together.

After eating, they went back to the van to wait for everyone to return. Bill got in and turned the key.

There was a single click, but the van wouldn't crank.

ULY
Tuesday Night

A white fifteen-passenger van towing a nice, enclosed equipment trailer was parked at the edge of a gas station parking lot. Both the trailer and the van looked brand new, but the van seemed to be having engine trouble since the hood was up.

The van had "The Church at Wesley Square—Savannah, Georgia" all the way down the side in neat black vinyl letters.

A mix of men's and women's voices softly talking and laughing drifted across the parking lot. A few people were standing around the van. They were in their tastefully coordinating but purposefully not uniform Sunday best.

Some of them had their shirts untucked or neck ties hanging loose. Some looked sleepy and were wearing big pink fluffy bedroom slippers. It was late evening—or early morning, according to how you think about it.

Uly thought about this for a minute. This was a church group with a van that wasn't working. He wanted to go to

Atlanta, not Savannah. But since their church was in Savannah, they might be going back that way. If he could catch a ride with them, it would at least get him farther down the road.

Uly was a smelly, not quite penniless, and unwashed hitchhiker with crusty, bloody wounds on his arms. They may not want to take him back to Savannah with them in their nice new church van, but it wouldn't hurt to ask.

A young man holding a screwdriver was peering under the hood.

Uly walked up more or less unnoticed and looked under the hood with him. This was a new van. There was almost nothing to see under the hood except brightly-colored ports for filling various fluids and an air-filter housing.

The man was trying to adjust something that looked like it was not significantly adjustable with a screwdriver.

He spoke to someone in the driver's seat. "Try it again, Marti."

She tried to crank it, but all it did was click.

Uly continued to look inside the engine bay. "At least it clicks."

The man with the screwdriver was younger than Uly, but his voice had that extra depth of both baritone and tenor resonance that some people who are singers or radio personalities have. "Do you know anything about cars, mister?"

"Yep. I've been fixing engines all my life."

Without a word he handed Uly the screwdriver and

walked around to the driver's side of the van. The woman scooted over to the passenger seat.

Uly was puzzled by the screwdriver. It had two tabs on either side of the head and didn't seem to be a tool that he could use in this situation, but he held onto it to give it back to the man. A cable was hanging loose under a black plastic housing. He pulled on it. One end was connected to something in the depths of the engine bay, but he found a plug on the free end.

He was certain it should be connected to the engine control module, one of the few components visible under the van's hood. He pushed the plug into an open port on the ECM. He knew that was the problem with the van when the plug clicked snugly into place.

Uly looked around the hood at the man who was now sitting in the driver's seat. "Try it now."

He cranked the engine, and it quickly settled down to a quiet purr. Then he came around to the front where Uly was struggling to figure out how to close the hood.

"Thank you so much!"

He shook Uly's hand with both hands. "We've been sitting here forever trying to call a tow truck or someone to come help us." He then quickly and easily closed the hood. "But it's so late we weren't having any luck."

"Well, there was a loose cable. I didn't do much of anything."

The choir members started climbing in.

"I'm Bill." He stuck his hand out for Uly again. "Driver and tenor in the choir."

He looked at Uly, waiting.

"Oh yeah. Hi. I'm Uly." He shook Bill's hand.

"Glad you came along. So, look, thanks again. We're running so late."

Some of the choir members started singing softly as Bill went back around to get behind the wheel. Uly followed him.

"So, um, Bill. I, um, I'm on my way back to Savannah."

"Oh, you are? Are you from there? You should visit us one Sunday morning."

"Well, the problem is I don't have a ride. Do you think? ... Would it be possible? ... I know I look like I've been running the streets. The thing is I ... I don't have a ride, and—"

"Say no more! You fixed our van! Hey everybody, make room for Mr. Uly. He fixed our van and needs a ride back down to Savannah."

Uly climbed into the van among a chorus of thank-yous, and comments like "you must be a mechanic," and such. Everyone was friendly and shared their snacks.

They got back on the road to Savannah, and some of the choir members broke into a song he had never heard before:

O, Lord, all your works,
Works move my heart.
Too many to count,
Count from the start.

O, LORD, all your deeds,
Deeds I declare.
No other like you. No, none!
None can compare.

Here I wait, LORD; hear my cry.
I know you'll help by and by.
In this pit, LORD, groans and shouts;
Turn to me, lift me out (Yes LORD).
Stuck in mud, LORD, I was bound,
But you set me on firm ground.

O, LORD God, you make,
Make me steady.
Sticky mud's gone now;
Now I'm ready

To sing songs you taught,
Taught to me new.
When I sing they'll see,
See me praise you.

Sing a new song! Praise!
Praise to you!
Hallelujah, hallelu!
Gonna sing a new song! Praise!
You taught me new.
Glory, glory! Hallelu!

On the road back to Savannah, the passengers and Bill quickly grew quiet. Uly was awake and tried to anticipate what could be next. He didn't want to impose on Bill or the other members of the choir any more than he already had. He also didn't want to go all the way back into downtown Savannah.

That's when he saw a sign for a hotel in the distance and decided this would be a good time to ask Bill to drop him off. Bill and a few choir members who were awake thanked Uly as he got out of the van in the parking lot of the old hotel. Then they continued down the road.

Uly didn't have near enough money for a hotel room, not even a cheap one off the beaten path, so he didn't bother to go inside.

He crossed the road and walked a hundred yards or so when he found himself standing next to the open gate of a large junkyard. Most of the name was missing on the plastic sign which had once been backlit, but the words "Auto Parts and Salvage" had survived.

A light was on in the shop at the back of a long row of junked cars. It seemed that someone was working late. They might have a couch in their office he could crash on.

In the darkness the old cars looked like a sea of motionless, black whales filling the huge lot, but the main drive to the shop was unobstructed by wrecks.

Uly walked toward the shop. The dirt drive—not gravel, but sand and mud holes—was long and curved around to a row of locked garage bays. A single lightbulb burned inside the building for security, but otherwise, it was locked up and quiet.

Walking around to the back of the building in the dark, Uly tripped and caught himself on a pile of car doors, causing a terrific clanging commotion. He half expected a Doberman to come thundering up ready to make a new friend—or whatever it is Dobermans serving on security at junkyards do. He didn't want to think about it.

In the deep darkness among the small sounds of night, surrounded by the shadows of nearby trees and the amorphous blobs of the junk cars, Uly shuddered despite a warm breeze. Bright stars twinkled, but the moon had set hours ago. Fear tweaked a nerve in his jaw and overwhelmed his thinking. He started praying and suddenly remembered a verse:

Don't be anxious about anything.

It was from a verse he didn't quite remember in Philippians that he had learned at Rachel's church. He thought for a minute but still didn't quite recall all of it. *In every situation God will guard your heart and mind.* He was leaving out more than he remembered. *Do not be afraid. In every situation, be thankful. God will guard your heart in Christ ...*

That wasn't it, but he felt a new confidence. He could still hear Mrs. Lucy sharing her secret to living a long life. "Trust in the Lord."

He explored some more. Around back he discovered that the shop was dark and locked up. Light from the lone security light burning inside wasn't finding its way into the junkyard.

No one was there.

Uly avoided another stack of car doors piled so high he wondered why they didn't fall. He tried to walk back around to the front of the shop, but that wasn't where he ended up. Instead, he found himself between more rows of cars, and he seemed to still be behind the shop.

Through a chain-link fence, he could see cars going by on the main road, so he decided to go back to the gate before he found out for sure if there was a junkyard dog there or not. But no matter which way he turned he didn't get to where he thought he was going.

He made it to the fence he had seen. The cars going by weren't on the main road. It was some other road behind the shop. There was no gate.

Ancient wrecks, classic delivery trucks, old school buses, and other hulks were stuffed against the high chain-link fence. Tough, serrated grass ten feet tall grew up between the cars, which were no longer in rows. Instead, they were stacked so tight they boxed Uly in on all sides. The sultry, motionless air had the sharp smell of rusting iron, rotting gasoline, and moldy vinyl. Thick weeds hid critters that scurried away as he walked.

Still carrying his two duffel bags, Uly squeezed down one row toward what looked like an old VW van with no front bumper—or doors, windows, or tires.

He resisted turning on his phone to use as a flashlight because the battery was too close to dead, and he would need it to call Rachel again for more money or to pick him up or something.

But he decided to use it to check the seats in the old van anyway. It would be better to use up the battery than lie down on a snake. It would be worth it to know if this was a place he could sleep until sunrise when he would be able to see how to get out of the old junkyard.

He checked the van's interior. "Good enough."

He collapsed on a bench in the back of the van, exhausted. After he rested a minute, the memory verse bubbled up:

Don't be anxious about anything, but in every situation, with prayer and petition and thanksgiving, present your requests to God. And the peace of God, which transcends all understanding, will guard your hearts and minds in Christ Jesus.

Uly considered this verse good news, and he quickly dropped into a deep sleep.

ULY
Wednesday Morning

A rhythmic clicking awakened Uly. Blue skies glared overhead and the hot sun was already cooking the rusty VW van.

Alarmed by the clicking sound, Uly scrambled out, facing the front door of the shop. A man with a baseball bat in one hand was walking toward him with a laborious gait accompanied by a click-clack, click-clack. He wore tennis shoes and white socks that collapsed around silver-colored old-fashioned prosthetic legs. Both legs.

The man click-clacked over to Uly and stopped at a respectful distance. "What are you doing here?"

He was bald and had the air of a man used to being answered when he asked a question.

Uly didn't answer.

"I said, what are you doing here?"

"I, uh ... got lost. I thought someone was here last night, so I went by the office and then I—"

The bald man launched a big black streak of tobacco

juice at Uly. "What do you mean 'got lost?' There's the gate right there!"

The man pointed to his right. In disbelief, Uly looked where he was pointing.

There was the gate right there.

Holding the bat in his right hand, he slapped the palm of his left hand with the side of the bat as he spoke. "You 'get lost' again and don't come back?"

Uly cringed more at the man's tobacco-juice-spitting accuracy than the threat of being beaten with a bat. He grabbed his bags and backed away. The man followed with a well-practiced hip-rotating shuffle, click-clacking and complaining. "I done had all my tools stolen once this year"

Uly turned to walk away, apologizing. "I'm sorry. I didn't mean—"

For some reason he couldn't quite put his finger on, Uly squared his shoulders and turned back to face the man. "I didn't steal any tools. I was just looking for a place to sleep. The only tool I have is this screwdriver."

He pulled the screwdriver Bill had given him from a bag and showed it to the man. Uly had forgotten to return it.

"That's not mine. All mine are new! And have orange handles."

"Okay, well ... it's not mine—"

"It's not! What did you do? Steal it?"

"No! No, I didn't—"

"Wait. Is that a number eight spanner bit?"

"What?" Uly said, looking at the odd screwdriver. "I don't know what it is. This man gave it to me last—"

"Let me see that."

Uly held it out to the man, who took it and looked at it closely. "It is a number eight spanner bit. Someone stole mine. I need it to tighten the set screws on my knee joints."

"Okay! Well, that's fine. You can have it."

While examining the screwdriver, the man unleashed another dark jet of tobacco juice. Then he looked back up at Uly, squinting suspiciously.

Uly hurried to the front gate, wondering why a set screw on a prosthetic would require an uncommon screwdriver. He wanted to ask the man about it but decided he had already overstayed his welcome. Uly looked back in time to see the Auto Parts and Salvage man click-clack back into his shop.

As he exited the open gate of the junk yard, Uly considered the road ahead. He decided to head south, but he didn't have a plan. Despite that, he found himself walking with a calm confidence that he couldn't contribute to his actual situation.

The sun had risen quickly and was a hot electric heater overhead. The blue sky was dark to the southeast. A light breeze had gradually gotten stronger. Looking at himself, he realized his clothes were covered in black, dusty mold and grime he had picked up from the bench in the old VW van.

Uly walked for about an hour in the hot sun as dark clouds scuttled in and the sky grew more threatening.

He looked and smelled terrible, so he decided to stop at the next gas station he came across to change into clean clothes from his bags.

He walked several miles, alternating between the pavement and the tall grass on the shoulder of the highway when cars came by. He stumbled over the sandy, uneven ground every time he had to step off the pavement. He gradually began to acknowledge a headache from the heat and dehydration.

At least there was a breeze.

The roads are long, flat, and straight in coastal Georgia. In the distance, a highway overpass bridge crossed the road. Well beyond the bridge there was an old sign swaying high up a pole next to a gas station. The gusty breeze was tinged with a hint of lightning-blistered air.

One or two great big drops of rain fell here and there, sizzling on the hot pavement. Uly picked up his pace in hopes of getting to the bridge before the bottom fell out.

The winds were getting stronger. He walked faster and then started running.

No luck.

A wind-blown downpour dumped out of the sky. Sheets of water whipped into him as he ran for cover.

A solid wall of water was cascading off the overpass, completely soaking him from head to toe as he ran under it. The thundering waterfall from both sides of the overpass was pierced by the cackling laughter of a homeless man perched on the sloping concrete of the berm under the bridge.

He had wild white hair, a short, scraggly beard, and a fissured face from years of living outdoors. He squatted high above the roadbed like a vulture watching Uly. An old grocery-store buggy piled with blankets and other items sat at the foot of the berm. The man stood up, tall, thin, and broad shouldered, but none too clean. Sharp blue eyes dominated his face behind thick glasses with black horn-rimmed frames.

He spoke clearly and loudly. "Jump back! Ha ha ha!"

His voice had the timbre of a tin can full of gravel. It echoed in the confines of the space under the bridge but was muffled by the downpour.

"Jump back! Ha!"

Uly looked at the man and wondered what to expect next.

Lightning popped nearby accompanied immediately by a scratching whip-crack of thunder.

The man stood, and then he squatted back down. He sprang up again and paced the top of the berm. He wasn't at all used to being around people. "Jump back! What do you lack, Umbrella Fella? White Cadillac!"

Uly had no idea what he was talking about. He put his bags down. Then he watched the man while trying to clear water out of his eyes.

Finally, the man shook both fists at the concrete bridge above and turned to look down at Uly while dropping into a dramatic stoop.

He yelled directly at Uly: "Jump back!"

"What? What do you mean?"

Uly finally realized he was telling him to jump back. He jumped away from the lane to the concrete shoulder as a black sedan rocketed through the waterfall and sprayed him with grimy road water.

Uly stood there stunned. Dirty water dripped down his face. When the shock of surprise wore off, he looked up at the man. "Thanks. I think. How did you ... ?" He paused, squinting at the man. "I didn't know a car—"

"Yep, yep," said the man as he skittered down the concrete berm to the roadbed in a practiced move.

He fumbled under an old blanket in the buggy, pulled out a ratty old towel, and held it out to Uly. "What do you lack, Umbrella Fella? Rain's done. Trade this towel for yo' umbrella." He spoke clearly and sanely.

Uly paused, looking at the waiting man. "How did you know I have an umbrella? I had forgotten about it."

The man repeated himself. "Rain's done. Trade this towel for yo' umbrella."

He stood there with his hand out, fingers twitching insistently.

Thunder rolled in the distance. Uly dug around in one of his bags. He pulled out the compact umbrella the grandmother had dropped outside the bus station two days before.

The man motioned again for Uly to give him the umbrella. Uly handed it over, and the man turned back to the rusty buggy to stow the umbrella.

Uly stood there watching the man, not knowing what to

think. "Thanks."

He dried his hair and wiped down his face and arms with the towel.

The man stood tall and then suddenly turned to Uly and spoke directly to him. "Cadillac, make yo' move! Ha ha ha!" He cackled. "Yep, yep."

Then he started pacing circles around the buggy, ignoring Uly.

"Whew!" he yelped in his tin-can voice a few minutes later, pacing some more.

Uly tried to hunker down into a squat to watch the man pacing and lurching around. Then stood back up because squatting caused him pain when it stretched his healing road burns from the bicycle accident.

The man crossed the two-lane highway under the overpass, mumbling and randomly whooping. He stood with his back to Uly, then turned dramatically. "Cadillac! Make yo' move!"

Uly was quite sure this man had more troubles than he did. He also suspected the man might not know it. But how had this guy known he had an umbrella or that a car was coming when it was raining so hard? And what was this about a Cadillac?

Uly watched the rain slowly subside. The solid waterfall pouring off the bridge overhead had given way to a broken, misty shower. The dark gray sky was beginning to lighten. Steamy mist rising from the roadbed competed with the rain that was still falling as the sun tried to break through. Another car whizzed by, harmlessly spraying the edge of the road.

As the weather cleared, the homeless man paced for a while, still mumbling to himself.

"I'm Uly, by the way."

The man didn't respond. A bird flew under the bridge with a flutter. Sunshine began to brighten the road. The cacophony from the bridge's waterfall had given way to the quiet sounds of gurgling water and dripping leaves on nearby trees.

"Cadillac! Make yo' move! Ha!"

Uly was startled by the sudden outburst. He looked up to see if another car was coming—maybe a Cadillac this time?

Uly tried to treat the man as if he had said something that made sense. "Nope. Don't see one."

"Yep! Yep! Whew!"

There were few cars on this stretch of road. There wasn't an on-ramp to the highway above. Occasionally a semitruck would pass thump-thumping on the bridge above. Down the road at the old gas station, a few cars had pulled in and parked while Uly waited under the bridge.

"Cadillac! Make yo' move!"

Uly looked at the man. "You wouldn't believe what I've been through over the last three days."

He started trying to have a conversation, but the man grabbed the handlebar on his rusty wire-frame grocery-store buggy and started pushing it across the road. He departed in the direction from which Uly had come.

He moved quickly down the road and then yelled loudly, "Ha-ha-ha! Cadillac!" Rather than finish the phrase, he looked back at Uly with a knowing grin.

Uly quietly mouthed the words, "Make yo' move."

The man hurried on down the road, pushing his rattling buggy in the post-thunderstorm sauna of the coastal Georgia heat.

CHUCK
Wednesday Late Morning

Chuck couldn't imagine anything better in his life right now than visiting his grandchildren. It was an absolute joy.

He was also ready to go back home to Dublin.

He had gotten up early and made coffee before anyone else stirred. He made it to his liking, about half as strong as Marti and Ted normally made it. Then he enjoyed the morning on the back porch while reading the devotion for that day from his well-worn leather-bound copy of Oswald Chambers.

Since the back of the house faced west, he couldn't see the rising sun itself, but it lit up the marsh and an immense live oak in the backyard. Live oaks don't tower—they sprawl. His grandkids loved to climb the tree's strong limbs which looped toward the ground and then curved back up.

He stared at the tree thinking about his devotional reading. A dry crust of resurrection fern coated the top of most limbs and stringy bundles of Spanish moss decorated the tree here and there.

Marti broke his reverie, poking her head out the French doors next to the kitchen. "Toast, Dad?"

His voice croaked because he was speaking for the first time that day. "Sure. You're up early. When did you get in?"

He stood, bones creaking and popping, and went inside to eat a piece of toast with Marti. She was scrambling some eggs to go with the toast. "Very late. We got in very late. We had van trouble."

Tabitha and Ted joined them.

Ted asked, "Trouble with the new van?"

"Yes. But a man who needed a ride just showed up out of nowhere and fixed it."

After they sat down at the table, they talked about things for a while: plans for what remained of the summer, upcoming birthdays, news about one of Ted and Marti's old high-school friends.

Chuck checked his watch. "I've got an appointment with Norm, so I have to get on the road by noon."

"Who's Norm?" Ted asked.

Marti began stacking everyone's empty plates. "He's Dad's insurance agent."

"I have to pay the insurance premium every six months." Chuck spoke in a tone that made it sound like paying car insurance premiums every six months was a situation unique to him.

Marti looked at Ted, smiling. "He likes to pay it in cash to Norm personally."

Chuck was defensive. "I could mail in a check, but I like for Norm to see that I'm still able to drive. He might start thinking y'all took my keys away from me if he doesn't see me every so often."

Marti mimicked her dad talking to Norm and deliberately stole another one of his lines. "'They done already put me in the nursing home.'"

Ted tried not to laugh. Chuck gave Marti his patented faux look of disapproval. Then Ted told them good-bye before leaving for work.

The boys finally found their way downstairs.

Mike gave Chuck a good-morning hug. "You are still going out on the boat with us again today, right, Pop?"

Gabe also hugged his grandfather as Marti spoke. "Y'all take Pop out on the marsh as soon as you can, boys. He has to get on the road early."

Later, his three grandchildren took him out in their john-boat for the second time that week. They called the path through the marsh grass a "creek," but to him it looked like open spaces randomly meandering between thickets of tall grass.

They all wore hats with wide brims, but the kids wore them in a way that made them look natural and fashionable. Mike and Gabe made expert paddle moves, guiding the boat at a rapid clip through the marsh. They were going fast enough to create a breeze.

Tabitha talked non-stop, explaining everything. "This is speedboat mode."

Gabe laughed. "We've grounded the boat at this speed before. It sticks in the mud good when you do that."

"Yeah, but that's been a while," Mike said. "We know the creek better now than we did back when we were kids."

Chuck was looking over the starboard side of the boat at the black goo on the banks of the creek. "I hope you don't ground us today. I don't think I can walk in that."

Tabitha agreed. "Nope. You'd be stuck good."

The expanse of marshlands between Tybee Island and Savannah is remarkably vast. All he saw was water and marsh grasses for miles and miles. Houses looked like tiny toys dotting a tree line in the extreme distance. Big anvil-shaped thunderheads marched in grids and rows across the sky much farther inland.

Gabe studied the sky. "Looks like rain."

Mike had been watching the water level. "And the tide is coming in."

Without any discussion, the boys subtly shifted their paddling pattern and turned the boat to start heading back home.

At some level, Chuck wasn't ready to go back to his own home even though he had been gone since Saturday. He considered this moment as close to perfect as he could imagine.

Back at the house, the kids helped him out of the boat. Chuck watched as they quickly put away their gear without any supervision. Then they helped him navigate the steps up to the back door.

He changed into clothes he had set aside for his ride home.

Then he had lunch with Marti.

"Is that all you're going to eat, Dad?"

"I think so. I'm not hungry."

The kids hadn't come in for lunch since it was still early. Chuck heard them shouting and laughing outside. Or were they arguing? It was all about the same much of the time.

He talked to Marti a few more minutes. Then they took their dirty dishes to the kitchen and made their way to the door. Marti held his elbow as he navigated down the long run of front steps.

About halfway down the steps, Marti realized they had forgotten something. She looked at Tabitha. "Run inside and get Pop's bag, please."

The twins were throwing a football dangerously close to his car. He didn't want to say anything about it, but he didn't like it.

Marti didn't like it either, but she didn't hesitate to say something. "Y'all stop that!"

Marti looked at the sky and then, with worry on her face, she looked at her dad. "You might hit some weather."

Chuck nodded and replied with an old-fashioned expression. "I'll drive 'tic'lar."

He knew Marti liked that word. It meant "particular" as in "I'll take *particular* care to drive safely." All that in one abbreviated old country word.

"You take back roads most of the time, don't you?"

Chuck nodded again. "Usually."

Tabitha placed Chuck's bag in the backseat of his car. She hugged him and tugged on the lapel of his blazer. "You dress so nice, Pop. And you smell like tobacco."

He was wearing a white button-down collar shirt open at the neck, a navy blazer with golden buttons, and breezy light chocolate-colored slacks with leather low-profile driving moccasins.

Chuck hugged everyone and then took a few more minutes saying his good-byes.

ULY
Wednesday Noon

Still under the bridge, Uly stood up, wriggled his hand into his soaking-wet jeans pockets, and sighed in exasperation. He had an ink pen and some change in his right pocket and exactly one dollar left over in his wallet. That was all the money he had. It wasn't far to the gas station, so he headed that way hoping to change clothes and get some food since it was lunchtime and he hadn't eaten anything all day.

As he reached the gas station, an old VW Beetle painted an iridescent purple tore into the parking lot with a spray of pea gravel. The muffled thump-thump of repetitive dance music boomed loud and clear as the driver opened the door.

Three women in short sequined dresses and high-heeled furry-topped boots got out of the car. Maybe they were going to a dance or an expensive club in downtown Savannah or they needed to make a snack run. It was hard to tell since it was noon on a Wednesday.

Uly found himself attempting to walk with more confidence and dignity than he felt. As he approached the group, he tried to wipe some of the water and grime off his face. He got gunk out of the corners of his eyes and tried to tame his crazy hair.

The ladies saw Uly from a distance and nudged one another.

One drawled out a long "hi there."

The driver closed the door behind her. "Whatcha doin', hun?"

Uly decided to be friendly. "Y'all look like y'all are ready to party … "

The third lady had a deep scowl. "Oh my! Uh-uh! What is going on with you?"

"Oh, my word, darlin'! You ain't right. What is up with that?"

They started laughing hard and scrunching up their noses while looking at Uly like someone had stepped in dog poo.

Then it got worse.

One started snorting and laughing uncontrollably.

They were guffawing so hard they dropped any pretense of being sexy. The women hooted with raucous laughter and backed away, letting Uly go into the gas station ahead of them.

He walked by, embarrassed and humiliated, not looking at them, not knowing what had made them laugh so hard. He hurried into the station, avoiding eye contact with the cashier. The laughter continued outside.

He went straight back to the deplorable excuse for a men's restroom. Looking in the mirror, Uly had no idea who was looking back at him.

His naturally curly hair usually had some body. This was different. He had dried his hair with the towel from the homeless man. Now it was a huge, greasy, matted, curly mess from rain and sun and from not being washed since Monday evening at Mrs. Lucy's bed-and-breakfast.

His face was streaked with four or five solid black lines running from the corners of both eyes down his face and neck. A black, oily smudge completely covered his mouth and chin.

Somewhere outside the door to the restroom, the Ladies of Savannah had followed him into the convenience store and were now howling with laughter and talking to the store's clerk about him.

He looked at his hands. His fingers were jet black on his right hand. He looked down at his pocket. The ink pen hadn't leaked—it had exploded. A huge black circle stained his blue jeans where the tip of the pen sat in the bottom of his front pocket. He pulled the greasy black mess of a pen from his pocket and threw it in the trash. He pulled out the handful of ink-stained coins and threw them in the sink.

Uly washed his hands and washed them again. Then he started trying to get the ink off his face. It was slow going. He was using all the hand soap in the little dispenser at the sink. A pile of inky paper towels was growing in the tiny trash can. He didn't care. He kept working to get the ink off his face.

The laughter had finally died down, and then he heard the women pull away in a gravelly scramble.

He washed his hair in the sink with a half-dozen pumps of the hand soap and dried it with the towel the homeless man had given him. His scalp still itched from sand-flea bites.

Finally, he peeled off his wet clothes, being careful not to reopen his wounds. He dried off as much as possible with paper towels. Then he put on the driest clothes he could find in his bags.

He spent well over an hour, trying to get ink off his face and getting cleaned up. He was thirsty, so he slurped up a few handfuls of the lukewarm, sulfurous water from the faucet. Then he walked out acting as though he had walked in a few minutes earlier.

The cashier eyed him suspiciously. He felt guilty for having moved into their restroom without paying any rent, so he used the black coins to buy some gum while mumbling a thanks to the clerk. She grimaced without ringing up the sale.

He walked out and stood in the middle of the parking lot, trying to decide what to do next. Where to go?

The chewing gum made him hungry. He searched for more of the beef jerky, but it was long gone, and he had eaten the Snickers bars a lifetime ago.

He finally decided to continue down the road in the direction that he thought would take him back to Savannah.

Uly walked a mile or so and passed a defunct car wash and a line of mostly empty stores in an old shopping center.

A busy tire shop was down the road from the shopping center. It was a local place with a regular wooden door and normal windows rather than modern store-front-style glass doors and windows. Customers were coming and going. The sound of air compressors and impact wrenches filled the air.

Uly was starving. A pizza delivery was in progress as he approached the store.

Improvising, he dropped his bags around the corner of the store out of sight of the front door. Then he followed the pizza guy inside. He sat in a chair in the waiting area near the entrance and kept his eye on the pizza.

The delivery guy pulled a large pizza box out of a black insulated padded case and set it on the customer service counter.

The tire-store clerk was wiry with stringy muscles that looked like he had thrown tires around for most of his life. He paid for his pizza while greeting Uly with a friendly, "Afternoon, what can I do for you?"

Uly adopted a confident tone. "Yes, let me get a quote on some tires for my ... " He hooked a thumb toward the wall with no windows to imply he had a car parked out there. He wasn't sure what he was doing, but he knew he needed to eat. Once again, he didn't want to be either a thief or a beggar.

"What size?" asked the clerk, taking a seat on a stool behind the counter.

"P225/75R16s," Uly rattled off quickly. Anything he could think of would do.

"All-terrain?"

"Yes."

The clerk rapidly pecked at a keyboard and studied a screen on the counter.

The front door opened and an old man wearing a blue blazer stepped into the tire shop office while holding tightly to the doorknob. He walked in holding some papers in his hand and asked if he could use a stapler. The clerk handed him an ancient one from which most of the seafoam-green paint had been worn by years of use.

Having organized and stapled his papers, the old man looked for a clear spot on the counter to leave the stapler. "Thanks for everything."

He placed the stapler on the counter between the computer screen and the pizza. The clerk was still looking at the screen. The smell of the fresh pizza made Uly's stomach rumble audibly.

The clerk glanced up at the man as he was leaving. "Anytime. Come back to see us, Dr. Chuck."

After a few seconds, the clerk looked up at Uly. "See if any of these will work for you."

He pushed on the corner of the flat screen, rotating it around for Uly to see. It would have cleared the top of the pizza box if the stapler hadn't been there. However, the screen pushed the stapler and the stapler pushed the pizza box just enough.

The pizza flipped off the edge of the counter and landed upside down on the concrete floor.

Splat!

Little bits of green peppers, pepperoni, onions, and black olives scattered, littering the floor around the box. Uly squeaked and jumped up in surprise.

The clerk squawked in alarm and ran around from behind the sales counter. There was the box, pizza, and all on the floor. Marinara sauce had splattered all around the box.

With a sigh he picked it up, dropping the box of scrambled pizza on the counter with a thud.

Then he opened the box. "Look at that mess!"

It looked like a greasy pepperoni salad with cheese stuck to the top of the box. Slimy, doughy triangles were folded randomly around inside. Floor grit and dust bunnies clung to the edges of the box, glued there with marinara sauce. The clerk pushed the ruined pizza away with a grimace.

"You want me to throw it away for you outside when I leave?"

"Yeah, I guess." The clerk shook his head, looking at the pizza with regret.

Uly quickly grabbed the box of tumbled-over pizza and hurried out the door before the clerk could say another word.

Once outside he disappeared around the corner to the parking lot on the side of the building where cars were being serviced. He was in time to see the man in the blazer who had borrowed the stapler shake another man's hand and walk over to an enormous white boat of a car.

Uly was busy trying to peel cheesy pizza goo out of the box and roll it all up into a great big feast for himself when he became aware of what he had seen.

Dr. Chuck was about to drive off in his white, slab-sided, two-door, classic Cadillac Eldorado convertible.

Uly paused with his mouth hanging open and the first piece of pizza halfway to his face. "Cadillac?"

Make yo' move.

A strange chill ran up his spine. His feet wouldn't move.

With a huge blob of rolled-up pizza in one hand, Uly snapped out of his momentary trance and ran across the paved parking lot, waving down the driver of the Cadillac as he was reaching the parking lot exit.

"Hey! Hey!"

The car stopped and the driver turned to Uly with a friendly smile. "What can I do for you?"

"Can I get a ride?"

"Where are you headed, young man?"

"Atlanta. I'm stuck here. No money. Trying to get back home."

"I can take you as far as Dublin and then you can go the rest of the way from there. That work for you?"

"Sure. Just one second please. Let me get my bags."

He ran to get his luggage and then ran back to get into the Cadillac with his bags and sloppy pizza roll.

Chuck introduced himself, dropping consonants and adding diphthongs in a lyrical, Southern dialect. "I'm going home to Dublin. Name's Charles. Friends call me Chuck. I've been here in Savannah to see my grandchildren."

ULY
Wednesday Late Afternoon

Chuck kept his eyes on the road while driving with his hands at the ten- and two-o'clock positions. "I noticed one tire was looking a little low when I left my daughter's house this morning. Larry said I picked up a nail somewhere."

Uly didn't know who Larry was, but Chuck had that familiar habit some people have of mentioning people he knows as if everyone else should know them too.

Chuck's twenty-foot-long, gleaming-white, two-door 1966 convertible Cadillac didn't feel like it moved down the road. Rather, it was as if the road moved under a motionless car. This illusion held despite some wind noise around the fabric of the roof. Because it was so hot, Chuck had paused for a minute to raise the convertible top back into place before they got on the road.

Chuck continued in his preacher's baritone. "I decided it was time for four new tires. Now I'm glad I got them. Makes the car look new, huh? Sue and I bought this car in 1976 when it was already ten years old, but it was like new then, and I like to take care of it."

Uly glanced around, searching the seat and floor for any errant crumbs of the pizza catastrophe he was still munching on.

After that, Chuck didn't start any more conversations. Almost an hour later, Uly twitched and wondered if he had been asleep. Seeing that Uly was awake, Chuck spoke again. "I have an appointment with Norm this afternoon."

Uly turned to look at Chuck . "Okay."

"He's my insurance agent. Stopping to buy tires has made me late for my appointment, so we need to go by there first before they close. Then I'll drop you off at Merlie's."

"Okay." Uly waited a beat hoping Chuck would explain. When he didn't, Uly asked, "So, who is Merlie?"

"Merlie's is a big truck stop next to the interstate. There will be truckers there who will take care of you and get you back up to Atlanta. Don't worry."

The ride from Savannah to Dublin wasn't short, but they were traveling in style. With the genuine Freon-powered air conditioner running and plenty of room to relax, Uly dozed off again. He woke up groggy with a headache, parched throat, and dry lips and was unable to remember the last time he had anything to drink.

Chuck had taken two-lane back roads all the way to Dublin. An occasional farmhouse broke the monotony of vast peanut or cotton fields and endless stands of tall longleaf pines. They stopped, turned, and passed an abandoned rusty gas station with a sign advertising gas at the ridiculously low price of 64.9 cents per gallon.

After traveling several more miles, they approached a traffic light at a busy intersection where Chuck turned toward civilization. He parked in front of a cinder-block building painted a light gray with an insurance agency sign on the door and smallish plate-glass windows.

Uly needed to stretch after the long ride, so he opened the car door, which almost spanned the entirety of the parking space beside the Cadillac, and was greeted by August in central Georgia: a blast of hot, humid air. Surprisingly, he wasn't sweating.

"Come on in where it's cool and wait for me in the waiting room. This'll just take a few minutes. Then I'll run you over to Merlie's."

Uly followed him in, feeling light-headed and not quite able to focus his eyes properly anymore.

A brass shopkeeper's bell announced their entrance, cling-clanging from where it hung above the door.

A secretary greeted them.

Uly sat down in a creaky, rusting black vinyl-upholstered chair. Dingy curtains hung on a window overlooking the backyard. The secretary was settled in behind a long counter built into the wall. She slumped over her keyboard as she worked at a computer.

It occurred to Uly that this had been a long day, and he

hadn't needed to use the restroom, even when he was getting cleaned up at the gas station after the rain.

He started trying to inventory his recent liquid intake. He'd had a Coke the night before, courtesy of the grateful church choir, and a few swallows of water at the gas station almost six hours ago.

The summer heat had hit Uly hard that morning in the old van at the junkyard. The sun rises early and can be instantly stifling during the right time of year in Georgia.

By the time he had gotten to the overpass bridge to wait out the thunderstorm, he was already dehydrated. A headache had started before he met the homeless man under the bridge and had continued uninterrupted since noon.

How far had he walked from the gas station to the tire shop? He didn't know, but it was during the hottest part of the day. He had stopped sweating at some point during that walk. The humidity had been so thick following the thunderstorm that he hadn't noticed the dehydration.

Since Chuck had been in a hurry to get to the insurance agency office before they closed, he hadn't stopped once on the long ride from Savannah.

Now it was almost six p.m., and the secretary looked like she was getting ready to leave work for the day. The back door of the office was open with an all-glass storm door closed to keep the cool air in. A cat cautiously investigated a trash can in the backyard. A dying pecan tree littered the ground with limbs and little bunches of brown, dead leaves.

The secretary suddenly appeared next to Uly.

"Water?" She placed a bottled water on the side table beside his chair.

Uly looked at it for a moment. It was beautiful. Drops of condensation gathered and trickled down the outside of the bottle, pooling in a silver puddle at its base.

He reached for the bottle and opened it.

The cold water hit his throat and stomach with an expanding, hydrating, healing chill. Energy unfolded into all his muscles.

This one little bottle of water was a true blessing from God.

He waited a moment, afraid the dreaded "ice-cream" headache was about to hit him between the eyes. The moment passed with no pain.

Sounds he hadn't heard a moment before became sweetly audible: Chuck talking to the insurance agent in the back of the building, the young secretary typing on the keyboard at her desk, the hum of the air conditioner, a printer clicking as it fed paper through its rollers, and a small lawn mower somewhere outside.

Uly slowly stood up with renewed vigor. Something important had changed. His life was turning around.

He became aware of his surroundings. The office wasn't shabby. It was old and had been decorated in the 1950s with the most modern and fashionable furniture of the time. It had been maintained well and was not fashionably retro. Rather, this was original mid-century modern décor.

Uly spoke aloud. "I don't know how I know that."

The secretary didn't hear him. She stood and walked down the short corridor across from Uly and opened the back door to let the cat come inside. It was a beautiful, especially fluffy calico who greeted him with a melodic "Meow-dela-reow."

The humble cat made eye contact with Uly and slow blinked at him. He could hear her purring from where he stood.

He drifted down the short hall to the back door, past the calico as it sauntered by in the other direction. He stepped outside, finishing the bottle of water in one more long gulp.

A landscape team was clearing a branch away from the base of the pecan tree and finishing mowing the small yard. The late afternoon sun lit up the yard with a golden glow. The pecan tree, brightly lit on one side, glowed against a brilliant blue sky. Its dark green leaves created a perfect canopy of cooling shade. The tree was ancient and tall with a wide sun-dappled trunk. It reminded Uly of the painting of the tree of life from the book of Genesis in the children's Bible he had read as a kid while he waited in the dentist's office.

Squirrels chased each other twittering and scraping up the trunk of the pecan tree. He walked around for a moment, admiring the garden-like setting there at the back of the little office. A big wasp flew at Uly, dodged around him, and kept going.

A hummingbird hovered, drinking from a feeder hung from a narrow cable outside a window. It backed away from the feeder, hovered for a moment, and checked over its shoulder. Then the bird furtively dodged sideways to a different opening on the feeder. Another hummingbird arced down toward the first one at fastball speeds. Uly watched them spiral up and away like dogfighting fighter jets.

Quiet calm descended onto the little backyard once the feuding hummingbirds were gone and the landscape crew had left.

Uly walked around looking at their work. Neat, plump layers of pine straw mulched the well-tended flower beds. The sun was behind the trees. Uly didn't know how long he was out there enjoying how much he had been revived by a simple bottle of water. Time had seemed suspended while he began to enjoy life again.

Then he heard a car door shut and the car pull away. It was probably the secretary. Uly regretted not thanking her for the water. He decided it was time to find Dr. Chuck, so he walked around and ended up in front of the house next door to the insurance office. He crossed the yard to the office's parking lot. Only one car was still parked there, and it wasn't Chuck's Cadillac.

The secretary was locking up the office. She was genuinely surprised to see him. "There you are! We didn't know where you went. Dr. Chuck couldn't find you and didn't remember your name or know your phone number or anything. He said you were only riding with him as far as Merlie's, so maybe you went ahead and walked on or got a ride or something."

Uly stood there thinking about what she was saying, what it implied.

"I was looking at how nice your backyard is ... " He trailed off, dejected.

"Oh right. That's our neighbor's backyard. She keeps the front and back so yard-of-the-month, doesn't she?"

"Um, yeah ... "

"Anyway, I'm locking up here. Do you need anything?"

Uly could see the anxiety in her face and knew she was just being nice while hoping he didn't need anything.

"No. I don't think I need anything. But where is Merlie's? Actually, is there a hotel around here?"

She pointed, smiling. "Right there! Right there behind you, hun, across the highway."

Uly turned to look. In the far distance was a sign he couldn't read for what might be a hotel. It looked like it was at least a mile away. She wasn't going to give him a ride.

She checked the front door of the office to make sure it was locked. "They have a good restaurant next door." She walked to her car, still talking. "I like to eat lunch over there. They have good fried chicken livers, mashed potatoes and steamed cabbage on Wednesdays."

She opened the door and got in her car, turned the key, lowered the window, and then shut the door, talking the whole time. "Of course, the lunch special is over by now, but they have good food, and there are always folks headed north. Somebody will give you a ride for sure. You know what I mean?"

She was talking too fast and giving him a forced grin. "But anyway, hun, you'll be fine getting back up to Atlanta. Looks like you've had a real adventure. Take care, hun. You hear?" she said through her side window as she pulled out of the driveway—actually going in the direction of the hotel—in somewhat of a hurry before he changed his mind about not needing anything.

"Thanks for the water," Uly said to the back of her car a little sarcastically. He understood. She didn't give rides to strangers.

The sun was setting, but it was still high enough that it would be a while before it was completely dark. He set off on the short hike to the hotel trying to think what to do next.

It suddenly occurred to him that Chuck had driven away with his bags ... and his phone!

The joy he had felt after he drank the bottle of water drained out as he considered how much more difficult this made things. He had purposefully not used his phone so he wouldn't deplete the battery. Now he would have to find another way to call Rachel.

RACHEL
Wednesday Afternoon

"Hello?"

"Hi, Mom."

"Hey sweetie. Are you calling me from work?"

"No, no. I'm off now."

She had never called her mom from work, so now Rachel considered it likely her mom already suspected something was wrong.

"Is everything okay?"

Confirmation.

Rachel tried to be breezy. "Oh, yeah."

There was dead air for a beat. Her mom knew better. Rachel clarified. "I mean, I'm okay."

"But what?"

"But Uly called me—"

"Oh, my word! Can he not see—"

"Well, Mom—"

"No. It's time for him—"

"No, Mom. This time it's different. He was stuck in Savannah, lost, with no money and no job. He was supposed to call me when he—"

"Good grief—"

"But he never did."

She didn't want to admit to anyone that she had sent him money.

"Well, what's new!"

"He was supposed to arrive in Atlanta on a bus yesterday morning. He wanted me to pick him up from the station downtown when he got here. He knew I wouldn't get off work until late. So, I thought I would pick him up last night, but I haven't actually talked to him. He tried to call, but I was at work and couldn't answer my phone right then and he didn't leave a voicemail."

"So, this is different then? And you don't know if he's here or not?"

"No."

"He probably got a taxi or something."

"He would have called me by now."

"So, he's coming here? Why is he coming here if he lives in south Georgia?"

"He lost his job or quit or something."

"Oh, that's too bad. You weren't actually going to pick him up from some nasty bus station downtown, were you?"

"Well, yes, that was the plan."

"I wish ... " Her mom didn't finish the thought.

"Me too, Mom, but he called twice, and I didn't want to keep ignoring his calls."

"It's just that—"

"What was I supposed to say? 'Uly, you're no longer a part of my life. Why are you bothering me with your stupid drama?'"

"Well, yes, that would work."

"Mom."

"I know you can't say that to him."

"No, I can't. So ... "

"Be careful down there. I'm sure you'll be fine."

"It's not that bad, Mom."

"Well, but ... "

"The thing is, I haven't talked to him, so I don't know where he is or what to do. I needed to talk to somebody about all this. And, honestly, you're more understanding about it than Robert or my friends at work."

Her mother laughed, breaking the tension. "Well, honey, I don't have any answers. Please let me know what happens, okay?"

"Okay, Mom. Love you."

"Call me. Let me know if I can help."

"I will. Love you. Bye."

"Bye, sweetie."

Rachel sighed and sat down in her living room, reminiscing.

Family was everything to her mom, who had been born in

Mexico. She insisted her children participate in every conceivable tradition in both Mexico and the States.

Her dad had started out as a farmer before becoming a residential real estate developer as the suburbs of Atlanta encroached on the farmland in DeKalb County during the last decades of the twentieth century. He was flexible like that.

She smiled thinking about how DeKalb County citizens said the name of their county. She didn't consider "duh-cob" or "dee-cab" correct. Her dad said it was only correct when pronounced "dee-kalb," with a vocalized *l*, and she agreed with him.

But she wasn't dogmatic about it. She had too many friends and acquaintances with different ways of doing things and ways of thinking about everything to insist on one way. The international mix of the population in DeKalb County resulted in large groups of people who, it seemed at first, had little in common except soccer, "fútbol" to them and some variation of the word to most of the world. Many of them followed American football, but they truly loved watching and playing soccer.

When they met at a World Cup viewing party, Uly had been neither shy nor especially confident. He had a sophisticated minimalism about him, a simple way of looking at things and a pleasant demeanor she found charming. He spoke casually about working hard without bragging.

This candor and humility wasn't at all like many of the men she met, and she liked that.

She *had* liked it, past tense.

Now, being uncharitable, she considered Uly to be oblivious and unmotivated. He was "simple" in a way that wasn't good.

He had told her about how he had worked hard to get beyond a stretch of teen years when he had been prone to follow the crowd, then leave it to follow a worse crowd. She appreciated that; it was part of what was good about him: his ability to see the need and choose a different path.

After they dated for a while, he started talking about moving for a better job. She had an excellent job she would not leave, so ultimately they broke up. He didn't move. They got back together.

Her mother didn't approve of him because she, not at all secretly, wanted Rachel to meet someone at work, preferably a nice doctor.

Then Uly did move.

Her mother liked him better once he was no longer part of the picture.

Rachel took a deep breath and sighed again, feeling a sense of loss.

That had been months ago, before Uly started calling or texting her from Albany randomly. She had told her mom she heard from Uly occasionally.

That didn't go over well with her mom, who made it clear that she did not get it. She didn't understand what Rachel saw in Uly.

Rachel didn't understand what she saw in Uly either.

She grabbed her phone and looked at it to check the battery and to make sure the ringer was turned on. She didn't want to miss his call.

RUSTY
Wednesday Evening

It had started getting dark outside. The storage area of Rusty's trailer was dark. It was now empty except for one box that remained to be delivered. The space was cluttered with pallets and protective cellophane wrap wadded up and mixed with large rectangles of corrugated cardboard. Most of this clutter came from the packaging around the big three-door refrigerator Rusty had delivered to Merlie's.

It had been a long two days. He had left Chattanooga early Tuesday morning, picked up the refrigerator in Marietta, made deliveries in Atlanta, and drove to Macon. He had cleared out the sleeping unit by this point, so he was able to sleep in the trailer that night.

On Wednesday morning, he had made several deliveries to churches in downtown Macon and then one more to a locally owned gas station off the interstate on the way to Dublin. A young employee accepted the delivery. He was confused when Rusty mentioned he wasn't heading back to Chattanooga yet.

"What do you mean 'install' a free-standing refrigerator on wheels? Can't you just roll it in and be done?"

"No. I have to get it off the trailer and all that." Rusty left as quickly as possible without explaining what "all that" included. Then he made the hour drive to Dublin to deliver and install the refrigerator.

Simply removing the pallet from the bottom of the heavy appliance had taken strategy, tools to remove the bolts holding it in place, and nearly an hour of his time.

Then he had to unbox it, remove the old refrigerator, move the new unit in, spend over an hour moving the free-standing ice maker two inches, install the casters, take all the packing materials out of the interior of the fridge, install the shelves, make sure it worked, load the old refrigerator into his trailer, and clean up.

Merlie didn't want him to use her dumpster for the packing trash, which made sense because it would have taken up too much room.

Now he was wandering around in the dark of the trailer, tripping over cellophane wrap, trying to find a tool he needed to install the coffeemaker because he still hadn't gotten to it.

Can't you just roll it in and be done?

Rusty mumbled a response to his memory. "All the work is in that one little four-letter word, *just*."

He was tired and hungry and had started to needlessly dwell on something stupid and negative. He needed a break, but he still had work to do.

"Rusty?"

"Yeah?"

Ant was standing at the back of the trailer. "You want some supper?"

"That would be great."

"What you want? I can put in a word for you to the cook!"

"Scattered, covered and topped," answered Rusty, trying to be funny by using Waffle House lingo.

"You got the right cook, wrong kitchen," said Ant, "How about the Captain's Platter? We got in some fresh shrimp this afternoon."

"That'll work."

"I mean, our shrimp are always fresh ... It's just that these are this-afternoon fresh, and our usual shrimp are yesterday-morning fresh."

Rusty wasn't listening anymore. "Okay."

"Give me about ten minutes."

Rusty went to the opening at the back of the trailer. "Hey, Ant. How critical is it to install the coffeemaker before morning?"

"Hold on. I'll ask Aunt Merlie."

Rusty climbed down out of the back of the trailer and closed the doors. When he returned from washing his hands at the hand-washing station in the kitchen, Ant was lifting a big basket of fried fish, shrimp, potato wedges, and hush puppies from the deep fryer. He dumped the basket into a stainless-steel pan with a grate in the bottom.

Merlie popped in holding a small bowl of coleslaw she had pulled out of the serving fridge.

"Rusty, do you have time to install the coffeemaker before you get back on the road in the morning?"

"Sure."

"That's fine then. We can go one more morning without it since it's not the weekend. The restaurant gets slammed on the weekends!"

They talked a while longer while Rusty ate in an employee break room at the back of the kitchen. Then Rusty thanked them for supper and pulled his truck out of the way before climbing into the sleeper unit. He was exhausted, but it was too early to go to bed. He called Meg to stay in touch.

CHUCK
Wednesday Evening

Chuck parked at the assisted-living facility. As soon as he got out of the car, he saw the bags in the backseat. Then when he got into his apartment, a light was blinking on his landline phone's physical answering machine, indicating a message was waiting. It was from the secretary at the insurance agency office telling him about seeing the young man who had been with him. When he finished listening, he called Ant, who answered right away.

"Ant? Are you busy?"

"Hey, Brother Chuck! Just washing up—closing the kitchen. What can I do for you?"

Chuck told him about giving a ride to the young man whose name he couldn't remember. Ant was banging pots and pans and running the commercial dishwasher. "You don't think he found a ride already, do you?"

"I don't know. Norm's secretary called me. She said she talked to him when she left work. He was wandering around in the next-door neighbor's yard."

"That's odd."

"I guess he could find a ride any time. I mean … So, it's possible he's already found one." Chuck was tired and didn't want to talk any more.

But Ant was a talker. "So it makes sense he might find his way over to the Waffle House tonight if he hasn't found a ride. I see everybody that walks in overnight. You wouldn't believe the stories—"

"That's right. That's what I was thinking—wanted to give you a heads-up."

Ant thanked Chuck for the information and agreed to be on the lookout for a young guy traveling on foot who looked like he might need some assistance. That didn't sound like it would be too difficult.

ULY
Wednesday Evening

After leaving the insurance agency office, Uly walked aimlessly over to the hotel the secretary had pointed him toward and into the little registration office. It wasn't cool inside. A feeble air conditioner in a window chugged loudly against the heat in the parking lot.

At the registration desk, an older teen boy ignored Uly. He was perplexed by something he was trying to do at the computer. "Be right with you."

He still didn't look up. "How many?"

Is he playing a video game?

"Um. All I need is one night."

The kid glanced up at him with a bored expression. "How many?"

Then he stared at Uly, waiting for an answer, assessing him, knowing he didn't have enough money, already deciding what he was going to do.

"Well, so, the thing is. Um ... is there any way I can ... Is there something I could do around here? You know?"

Uly paused and then spoke fast and desperate. "Can I work for a room? Just one night?"

"No."

No emotion.

"It would ... It's only for—"

"No."

Still blank.

"I thought maybe ... "

"No."

It was a simple, bored no. Then he blinked at Uly and waited.

"Please help me out here, buddy."

"No."

He didn't bother to shake his head.

Uly quizzed. "Nothing?"

"Uh-uh. It's not allowed."

The boy frowned slightly, giving the first hint of emotion.

Uly paused. He stood there a long time saying nothing. Most people would be uncomfortable with a pause this long. The clerk looked at Uly, unintimidated by his long, long pause, and waited a beat before looking back at the computer screen.

Uly turned to leave, irritated, knowing he had lost. "Okay."

"Sorry, dude." The emotionless clerk wasn't sorry.

Uly shoved the lobby door open angrily, but it was one of those commercial doors that will only open slowly no matter how hard you push, so it robbed him of the chance to storm out. It struck Uly then how tired he was and how late it had gotten.

He walked toward the highway, defeated, and then doubled back to the side of the hotel, a tiny bit of hope building up there.

There weren't many cars in the parking lot. The place had to be mostly empty. Perhaps a housekeeper would take pity on him and let him into a room. He walked all the way around the perimeter of the three buildings that made the U-shaped hotel without seeing another soul.

The place was a dump. Not one square of concrete sidewalk was fully intact without cracks or crumbling curbs. Each room had a big plate-glass window. Every one of them was cracked or fogged or dirty.

Eight-foot sticks of rusty iron pipe in a cluttery pile next to the door of one room marked an ancient construction project that had gotten stalled at some point in the past. Uly looked at the pipes, considering the amount of noise he would make. He was extraordinarily tempted to pick up one of them to break into a room through a window.

He sighed and turned away. There was a line he didn't want to cross. He was no longer a teenager who didn't give a thought to what would happen next. Instead, he was trying to imagine potential consequences of his actions. His options were limited, but that didn't mean it was a good idea to start vandalizing property.

He saw snack and Coke machines next to ice machines in the covered open-air passageways between each building.

A hand-lettered sign in black marker on humidity-rumpled copier paper taped to each machine with multiple layers of yellowing and cracking strips of tape stated, "Exact Change Only."

He was hungry and wished he had some change. He had a single one-dollar bill remaining, but no change. Knowing those old coin machines would most likely steal his money made him feel better.

He found an empty pool with a boarded up tiki bar beside it. The interior of the bar was used for storage now. Broken-down outdoor teakwood furniture sat near the boarded-up bar. The wood was so old it had aged to a crusty, splintering gray. It had once been decked out with Hawaiian-patterned outdoor cushions because there was one old cushion, drooping and faded, propped up behind the tiki bar. It was caked with years of pollen. On the bright side, it didn't seem to be too moldy.

The sky was the twilight deep blue of a long summer day. Some of the day's heat had given way to mosquitoes making high-pitched humming runs past Uly's ears. Bats chased them down, flicker-flapping around the old pool deck.

Hoping he wouldn't step on a snake in the dark, Uly fished the grungy cushion out from behind the tiki hut and dumped it on the creaky old teakwood sofa frame. He gingerly lay down, half expecting the old furniture to collapse.

Uly lay there hungry, homeless, jobless, and penniless. He caught himself not breathing, stuck in a long, unblinking stare that accompanies a feeling of numbness. He thought about how quickly he had gotten to this point. He was disconnected without his phone. He wasn't sure how to get in touch with some people he was close to. It's not like he had a bunch of phone numbers memorized.

He didn't bother to swat at a mosquito that buzzed his ear.

Not knowing what to do next, he dwelled on the unpleasant but persistent doubt that accompanied feeling sorry for himself.

His wounds from the bicycle accident still felt fresh. Mrs. Lucy's advice drifted into his thinking, "Trust in the Lord." He decided to pray.

ULY
Thursday Morning

Then it rained during the night.

A brief downpour soaked him to the bone in the middle of the midnight. He moved his outdoor sofa cushion to a covered breezeway when it started raining. Uly was good and wet when he finally gave up trying to get some sleep. Though the sun would rise soon, it was still dark. For the first time since he left Albany four days earlier, he was cold.

The restaurant next door to the motel wasn't open yet, but there were lights on in a Waffle House down the road. The yellow glow looked warm and inviting. He walked toward it with squishing shoes and no plan.

When he got there, he entered the restaurant. It was a minute or so after six a.m. The diners included an early morning crowd of truckers, farmers, and commuters. Still feeling sorry for himself, Uly imagined they all had fulfilling jobs and happy homes.

Uly held the door for a man who was leaving. He was

around Uly's age and was wearing a Waffle House shirt. A long scar from his temple to his chin rippled as he spoke.

He was talking loudly and laughing at someone behind the serving counter. "No! Uh-uh! You don't know nothin'! It's boring here when it rains at night. I mean nobody at all!"

The woman behind the counter responded to the man with the scar. "So, that's why you got all this cleaning done then, huh?"

The man replied with a good-natured rebuke. "Don't start! This place was spotless when you came in!"

Uly—no phone, no clothes except the ones he was wearing—was cold, wet, and broke. This guy might be a last chance. He had met people who could be heartless, scolding, bullying, thoughtless, and flippant. "Is there a truck stop around here where I can hitch a ride to Atlanta?"

"Yeah, sure buddy."

But Uly had met others who were casually helpful, willing to do anything for other people as if it were nothing.

Ant held the door open for Uly. "I can run you up to the truck stop at the next exit."

Uly followed the scar-faced man to his old two-seater, two-wheel drive Toyota Tacoma truck. The dark blue paint was faded and mostly didn't peel off due to the layers of grime and an ancient pollen coating. The windshield had two more-or-less clear overlapping arches surrounded by opaque regions of uniformly untouched encrustations that defied wind and rain.

The man's scar writhed as he talked. "I'm a cook at Waffle House every night. Then I go home, sleep, and go back to work at Merlie's. I cook over there for the supper crowd. Then I come back here to the Waffle House for an overnight shift. My fiancée works over at Merlie's too. I'm Ant, by the way." He extended his hand to Uly.

"Uly."

"I've got this old thing to get me back and forth, but it ain't like nobody aspires to own a little truck, right? Of course, some people want new and shiny things if all they've ever had is hand-me-downs and leftovers," Ant opined.

Uly got in the truck. Inside, it smelled like old French fries and mold. Ant never stopped talking as he pulled onto the interstate. He spoke with a quick Southern accent.

"My aunt and uncle own Merlie's Truck Stop, and they've got money, so they can afford to have one more cook they don't need." Ant laughed at his own joke.

Uly's attention drifted as Ant talked, telling all kinds of tales like Uly was an old friend.

"And right then my dawg went crashing through the living room and smacked into the sliding glass doors so hard I was afraid he was going to break the glass."

Ant unspooled his words in a continuous stream of consciousness. "That's how I got this scar. Most people ask me about it unless they don't, then they never do, some people are like that. My buddy hit a baseball through his mama's sliding glass door and it was locked and glass was everywhere.

There was this one big piece we didn't notice still in the frame at the top of the door and to get in we had to unlock the door so I reached through and unlocked it and this big ole piece of glass shook loose and fell so fast I didn't realize what happened. I barely felt it at first, and then I realized it had, like, cut my face off. But sometimes I tell Waffle House customers, 'I won the knife fight and you should see the other guy!'"

Ant, laughing at his own joke again, slowly brought Uly back around to paying attention. Ant took the next exit where he pulled into a large truck stop next to the interstate.

"When you go inside, ask for Nancy over in the restaurant area," Ant said, handing Uly a twenty-dollar bill.

Uly was amazed at Ant's generosity. "Okay. Thanks, man!"

Ant gave Uly a conspiratorial smile. "Just order by saying 'toast and coffee' and pay with that twenty. Leave all the change for a tip."

Uly got out of the truck. As Ant started to leave, a waitress was already holding the door open for Uly. She gave Ant a sweet little twiddle-fingers wave as he pulled away.

"Where you headed from here?" she asked nicely.

She forgot to call me "hun."

Aloud, he answered, "Atlanta, if I can get a ride."

"Don't fret. Not a problem. Have a seat. I'm Nancy. 'Toast and coffee' coming right up."

Nancy was on a mission.

Uly wasn't sure how this had been worked out. He hadn't needed to order toast and coffee. There seemed to be a network of some sort in this town.

A minute later a bear of a man eased into the booth across the table from Uly. He had a gray ponytail and neatly trimmed beard. His voice was quiet but with that rumble of someone who could be heard over a train engine if he needed to be.

"Rusty," he said, reaching across the table to shake Uly's hand. His hand completely engulfed Uly's and felt like an old dry leather glove over steel pipes.

"I'm Uly."

"That's my truck," he rumbled, nodding toward the window at a short-nosed Mack parked outside. It was clean but well-used with a modest trailer.

"I'm a one-man show. No company rules against giving rides to folks in need," he scoffed, contemptuous of bureaucracy.

"I deliver supplies and equipment all over. This is the end of my route for this trip, and then I'm headed back to Chattanooga. I can take you most anywhere in Atlanta. Nancy said that's where you want to go?"

"Yeah, that's right. Can I use your phone on the way?"

"Sure."

Nancy arrived with two big plates loaded with scrambled eggs, more than enough bacon, grits with a big dollop of butter in the middle, and biscuits busted open and covered with country gravy and sausage. She poured coffee into large mugs and left the pot of coffee with them along with silverware rolled in white paper napkins and plastic containers of coffee creamer, grape jelly, and butter.

"There's salt, pepper, and sugar on the table there for y'all, and if you need anything else, let me know."

After a few minutes, Nancy dropped by the table again. "Here's a voucher for a complimentary toiletries kit for travelers. It's not much—toothbrush and soap and such. It also includes rental of towels from the truck stop. Go by the retail desk over there with this note, and they'll give you your supplies. Showers are around the corner over there."

Nancy smiled at Uly and darted away.

Uly looked at Rusty. "That's too much for them to—"

"No. It's all covered by a fund they have here in this community. Ant, the guy that dropped you off here, and some of his friends started it."

Uly dug into his plate with gusto.

"What do you do for a living, Uly?"

"Nothing, now." He looked up at Rusty while crunching on crispy bacon, wondering if Rusty truly thought he had a job.

He decided Rusty was trying to start a conversation. "That's how I ended up like this. I quit my job and then took the wrong bus from Savannah, ran out of money ... I worked for a contractor who inspects poles for electrical companies."

Rusty stopped eating and put his fork down. "I didn't finish my work last night, so I still have a coffeemaker to install here this morning before we leave."

Rusty waited quietly.

Uly kept eating, talking around mouthfuls of food. "Okay.

I can wait until—" Suddenly he realized this was a job interview. "I can help! Do you want a hand with it?"

Rusty grinned and thought, *Correct answer.*

Aloud to Uly he said, "Sure. I can always use an extra hand."

After eating, Rusty pulled the old coffee machine from its location in the wait station. Uly helped. He mostly cleaned up as Rusty worked. The old coffeemaker needed to be drained and dried off, the wait station's countertop needed to be cleaned where it had been, the back of Rusty's trailer needed to be organized because it was cluttered with the packing materials from the new refrigerator. Then there was the inevitable spillage from the open lines of the water service outlets, even though the valves had been turned off, that fed the back of the coffeemaker.

Uly took care of all the cleanup while Rusty made sure the water and electrical services were working, the temperature was set properly, and there were no leaks inside the unit. Commercial versions of appliances are almost never plug and play.

Then Merlie made a pot of coffee in the new coffeemaker while Uly took a few minutes to get cleaned up after his ordeal.

The new machine was working perfectly, so Rusty prepped the truck and made sure it was ready to go. Uly joined Rusty at the truck as Chuck drove up with his convertible top down. "Hello, gentlemen."

Rusty spoke first. "Hi there, Dr. Chuck."

Uly did a double take. "You two know each other?"

"Hi, Uly. Ant called me this morning to say he found someone I had lost."

"You know Ant, too?"

"Oh yeah. We go way back. Your bags are right there where you left them."

Uly fished them from the backseat while Chuck explained he had alerted Ant to the possibility that he might find Uly looking for help in the area.

When Uly finally pulled the door shut on the passenger side of the Mack truck's cab, he took a deep breath and relaxed.

Rusty pulled onto the highway beside Merlie's and then up to the on-ramp to access the interstate.

"Do you have a plan, Uly? Can you drive a semi?"

"No ... and no."

"What about show up at my warehouse in Chattanooga if I need some help?"

"Well, yeah. I can drive up there if you need some help."

"It would be contract work. Nothing permanent."

"That's fine."

"I'll give you my number, so you can call me next week. I could use some help at the warehouse."

While they talked more about Rusty's business, Uly found his phone in one of his bags and plugged it into one of Rusty's charging cables. He thought about what he was going to say and hoped Rachel wouldn't be angry.

"Hey, I was able to find a ride and charge my phone."

"Okay. I'm not working today."

"Can we meet at The Varsity?"

"Um. Sure. When?"

"Around one?"

"Okay. Bye."

"Okay. Thank you. Bye." Uly was both disappointed and relieved that she had hung up before he could say anything else.

He slept for a while after he talked to Rachel. Two hours after leaving Dublin, they were in the Midtown district of Atlanta.

Rusty exited onto a busy surface street with four lanes of aggressive Atlanta drivers. Tall buildings with stores, banks, theaters, and restaurants on the ground levels lined both sides of the sidewalks.

One driver beeped a horn at Rusty for not dashing away when a traffic light changed to green. Rusty was annoyed. "You know, Uly, almost no one blows their car horn in this city except for people who don't know any better."

He might not have been fast enough for the one driver, but Rusty drove his big rig like it was a compact car. None of the other drivers felt the need to blow their horns at him.

With a friendly "Take care. Call me," Rusty dropped Uly off.

ULY
Thursday Noon

Uly stood in the parking lot at The Varsity for a minute before Rachel arrived. When he saw her, she was driving an extraordinary hot rod. He saw the car first and then realized it was Rachel. She had a grim look on her face.

The wheels were a dense arrangement of chrome wires that flashed like a huge, faceted diamond slowly rotating as she rolled in. The exterior sage-green paint of the hot rod practically glowed in the early afternoon sunlight under infinite clear coats.

A carefully detailed engine was painted a flat but shiny gray. The custom exhaust headers looping down off the top of the engine had long art-deco heat-sink fins cast into the metal. They were also gray, with bronze chamfered edges on the outside of the heat sinks catching streaks of sunlight, giving way to long white-silver exhaust pipes that dropped low to the side of the car.

The interior was upholstered in dark, deeply oiled, and

textured saddle leather. The glossy wooden steering wheel was a deep variegated charcoal showing off the wood grain. Chrome surrounded all the gauges and dials in dancing bursts of reflected sunlight as Uly walked toward the car. It was the most beautiful hot rod he had ever seen.

It was beautiful and so was Rachel.

Though it was a concours-perfect show car, Rachel had decided cars are for driving, and she didn't want to treat her Baby D like she was a trailer queen that couldn't get her tires dirty. This wasn't even its first outing, so why not pick up Uly in it?

She parked and opened the door without turning the car off. The exposed engine made a slow loping noise that turned into a gallop and then cycled back to loping as if it couldn't decide if it should stall or make a sudden mad dash for the highway with or without a driver. Rachel let the engine idle longer than necessary before turning the key to silence the beast.

Uly walked up to her as she got out of the car and shut the door.

They hugged, but it was brief.

Uly was shy, trying to be confident and act normal. "Hey. It's good to see you."

He wasn't looking at her as much as he was watching her to see what she would do.

She didn't say anything.

Then Uly couldn't help himself. He gaped and stuttered, gobsmacked by Rachel's ride. "How? Where did you get this?"

He shook his head. "A '32 Ford V8 hot rod, chopped and channeled! Wow!"

She stood there not responding, with one hand on her hip and the other slightly extended with her purse hanging from her forearm.

A light breeze snicker-snapped the lanyard on a flagpole nearby. Uly breathed deeply and held his breath.

Rachel looked at Uly, unsmiling, silent, waiting.

Awkwardly he said, "Thank you for wiring me the money the other day."

Still no response.

"And for coming to pick me up ... "

Still nothing.

"... and for answering the phone ... "

She tilted her head and hid her mouth with her hand. He was afraid she might leave.

"... and for buying me lunch at The Varsity."

If not exactly a full smile, at least she let a smirk cut through. "You are welcome!" She said with a waggle of her head as if he weren't welcome at all.

She presented the car to Uly with her hand like a model on a game show and said, "Say hello to Baby Deuce." One eyebrow arched.

He didn't hesitate. "Hello, Baby Deuce."

"Baby D is willing to drop you off someplace, presumably your mother's."

"That would be sweet."

Rachel grabbed Uly by the upper arm and propelled him toward the entrance of the restaurant. He willingly went along.

"You are not my very favorite person right now. In fact, ... "

The rest was in fast Spanish. She continued like that, with her cute summer sandals clip-clopping across the hot pavement as they made their way to the entrance near the tall Varsity sign.

They opened the front door and were confronted by the sight of the usual crowd: hundreds of customers chaotically jostling for a turn to place their orders.

"What'll ya have? What'll ya have?" rang out from the workers behind the counter.

Uly was home and thought he would be able to treat Rachel like he didn't take her for granted.

He looked at her and mumbled. "I can make this work."

"What?"

"I have a job offer."

"Make what work?"

Rachel's job gave her the extra income to make it possible to afford nice toys. She bought a fancy hot rod and then brought it out on the road, not to show off, but to allow Uly to see it and ride in it.

Uly chewed at the inside of his cheek. "Make us work. Maybe."

"There is no 'us,' Uly."

He stood there dejected.

"Do you know why I came to pick you up?"

"No."

"It's not just to help you. It's not just to be nice."

"I don't—"

"Do you remember back when you talked about your day, and I talked about mine, and we shared what was going on with each other?"

"Yeah. That was—"

"That's important. That's what I want. I want to share my day with you, Uly. Not just once a month."

That was a good sign. He now knew he was willing to be there for her, however inadequate he might be at that, and share his days with her.

Uly looked at Rachel. "Thank you for coming to get me. And for letting me ride in Baby D."

She gave him a look he couldn't quite interpret.

He continued. "You know I don't speak Spanish. But that's probably for the best."

He needed to decide what he wanted to eat before he got yelled at by the Varsity clerks. They like their customers to make up their minds quickly or get out of the way.

Rachel ordered using The Varsity's lingo. "Hot dog all the way with strings and Coke."

She moved aside quickly. Uly looked at her. She had already ordered. She was independent. She didn't need him.

That was for the best, too.

EPILOGUE
George, A Year Later

Uly had worked occasionally for Rusty, but he needed something more permanent. Rusty had a friend down in Cherokee County, north of Atlanta, named Ray-Ann, who owned a landscaping company. He had put a good word in for Uly, and Ray-Ann hired him.

After a few weeks, she asked him to work with a guy named George, who had been working construction, because she thought they would make a good team.

George lived in an apartment in Woodstock, one of the small towns in Cherokee County. His place was a random assortment of rooms in an old house with three other apartments in it. The carpet smelled like the previous occupant had an inside cat but not an inside litter box.

The plumbing was old and hammered spontaneously when he turned on the faucet. It was sure to release a slug of water made brown by the iron and whatever else turns supposedly good tap water brown.

Because tough, plastic, sports drink bottles are sturdier than the ones for other bottled drinks, he saved them to use as water bottles.

Each evening he filled two bottles about a third full of tap water and then froze them. The next morning before work he filled them with water. By the time he wanted something to drink, he had a cold bottle of ice water. The bottles fit neatly into an old book bag he took to work, along with a change of clothes and some lunch.

After a couple of months of working all around the northern suburbs of Atlanta, George and Uly were assigned a special job for one of Ray-Ann's friends who lived in south Georgia.

The morning of their trip, the water in George's apartment was especially yuck. Since he wanted extra water at the job site, he filled his bottles with the brown water anyway.

When he left his apartment, it was still pitch-black night. He could tell it was going to be a particularly hot day because it was already muggy before the sun was up. It would be worse in south Georgia.

When George arrived at the garage, Uly was already there. "Morning, Uly,"

Uly looked up from checking the oil in the fifteen-year-old company truck they had been assigned. He closed the hood. "Morning, George. I'll drive."

"Alright, I'll navigate."

They departed before the first hint of dawn. Uly always

drove all vehicles, including old trucks, like they were sixties muscle cars in a midnight street race. By the time the sun brightened the sky from purple to blue, they had been on the road less than an hour, but they had already traveled over sixty miles and were well south of the Atlanta airport.

The air conditioner in the truck was blasting cold air until it wasn't.

George adjusted the controls without any success.

"The compressor seized up." Uly sounded like he had been expecting it to happen.

George knew from experience that Uly knew about cars, so he was no doubt right.

Uly glanced at George with a wry smile. "Why don't you call Ray-Ann to see if we can get a different truck?"

"She likes you better. Why don't I call but let you talk?"

Uly grimaced. "I might freeze up and agree with her."

George shook his head. "No, you won't."

"She'll pause for a long time. I'll speak. Then I lose. You know, I've told you this before, 'The first one to speak is the loser.' You know that, right? If you're in an argument with someone and you want to win, don't speak again once you're done. First one to speak is the loser."

"You mean like right now?"

Uly didn't respond.

So George called Ray-Ann to request permission to turn back and procure a new ride. He already knew it was futile to ask for another vehicle, but they needed to let her know that the truck's air-conditioning had stopped working.

"Hi Jen, is Ray-Ann in?"

Jen was Ray-Ann's secretary and always answered the phone.

"George?" It was Ray-Ann.

Jen had transferred the call instantly while also conveying who was on the line. It didn't seem possible to do it that quickly, but that was Jen for you and the only administrative associate Ray-Ann would not have fired within a week.

Ray-Ann was always to the point.

Her husband had died years earlier, and she had inherited the business he had started. She hadn't had any part of it until that week. No interest at all. It was her husband's company. She had stayed busy with volunteer work at church and in other community organizations where she had developed a knack for getting things done without running off the other volunteers.

In other words, she was a certifiable genius.

Since she had some skills and lacked any other source of income, she made the new situation work by sheer willpower and sense of purpose. She also had a good-natured honesty and an easy laugh that won her points with her employees. But she didn't repeat herself, and she didn't waste time. Which was exactly why George didn't want to call.

In the face of the calamitous failure of the most important part of the whole truck, Ray-Ann laughed and told them not to be late getting to her friend's property in south Georgia.

"You can work on your perseverance," she said cheerily. George knew this was a Bible reference and scowled.

It was already too hot in the truck and the sun had barely risen.

"Anything else, sweetie?" asked Ray-Ann. She was sincere; not sarcastic.

"No. That's all—" *Sweetie.*

"Thanks for letting me know about the air-conditioning in that truck. Have a good one. Y'all call me if you need anything else," she finished from her air-conditioned office.

Later that morning, the work they were doing wasn't fancy or difficult, but there was plenty to do, and they were below the gnat line. They had driven far enough south that they were in the area of Georgia below Macon where gnats mercilessly annoy anyone outside at that time of year.

At lunch time, Uly pulled the truck under the shade of a tall oak. They sat on the tailgate in what they hoped would be a cool location, but the humidity averaged out the temperature and it was as hot in the shade as it was in the sun.

That's when George dug out one of his recycled bottles of water. He held it up to the light, considering the brown lukewarm water inside. "I could use a nice cold bottled water right about now."

Uly chuckled. "That reminds me of a story I'll have to tell you some time."

They worked later than usual to take care of everything the customer wanted done. As they were heading home, they stopped for gas at a Stuckey's. When they got to the on-ramp, Uly punched the old truck's V8, rocketing them back onto the interstate with a throaty roar. As they merged into the moderately heavy traffic, Uly started laughing again.

George looked over at him. "You're thinking about your bottled-water story."

"Yeah, I am. A while back I took a job down here in Albany."

George was listening to Uly over the whipping blast of outside air blowing into the open windows.

"That was before Rachel and I got married. She had her nursing job. She's smart and didn't want to leave it. She wanted to stay together, but I didn't know how that would work. I was stupid really. I left her for a job inspecting power poles and then tried to act like I hadn't actually left."

"That sounds like you."

Uly scrunched up his face at that comment. "Anyway, one Friday afternoon as I was leaving work they told me I had been assigned to a crew that was going to Savannah."

George looked confused. "What does that have to do with a bottle of water?"

Uly smiled. "I'll get to that."

THE END

Afterword

My father, Paul B. Williams, was an extraordinary man. He was an entrepreneur, fish farmer, marathon runner, primitive archer, woodworker, and a loving father, husband, brother, and Christian leader. You can read more about him on my website at BooksByTravis.com.

In the summer of 2013, my dad lost the ability to say the letter *r*. I suspected he had suffered a mini-stroke that damaged a nerve controlling the tip of his tongue.

It was much worse.

In February 2014, he was diagnosed with ALS (also called Lou Gehrig's Disease). The disease progressed quickly, and he died in November of 2016.

After he was diagnosed, my mom and dad traded in their car to purchase a wheelchair-accessible van. This gave them the opportunity to participate in everyday activities, attend church, go to doctors' appointments, and travel to their favorite vacation destination, Gulf Shores, Alabama.

Daddy had always fished off the pier at Orange Beach

there in Gulf Shores, and he didn't stop when he could only fish from a wheelchair with Mama's help.

After Daddy passed away, Mama frequently thought about what she could do to help individuals with ALS. She knew a man with ALS who was in need of an accessible van. She had also been wrestling with how best to honor my father's memory. The ALS Association chapter in Georgia had been an extraordinary resource for our family. The people there are truly dedicated to helping others.

All of this was heavy on her heart, and she had been praying about it.

One day when she was driving home after buying groceries, it occurred to her that all ALS patients and their families have a considerable need for accessible transportation because that is one of the most important ways ALS patients maintain their quality of life for as long as possible. Certainly that had been what my father had experienced.

My mom had the idea to provide transportation to ALS patients and their families for any reason at no cost to them. She didn't want to limit the service to medical needs or short trips. She decided to call the ALS Association to ask if her idea was doable. They thought it was.

In 2017, Linda Williams, our family, and the Georgia chapter of the ALS Association created the Paul B. Williams ALS Transportation Program. Through the program, individuals and their families living with ALS in Georgia can request to use an accessible van at no cost to themselves, for any purpose, for short trips and long ones, in-state or out-of-state. Alternatively, they may request a ride from local vendors for short, nonemergency trips.

Because the program is administered through the state ALS Association, it benefits from their nonprofit status and fund-raising efforts. All costs incurred by the program for van rentals, travel assistance, and even vehicle modifications and grants toward the purchase of a van are borne by private donations.

One of my friends noted that the way in which the program provides help to people who are in need is mirrored in *Uly Quits His Job* by the help several characters give Uly. While that theme wasn't intentional, perhaps it was subconscious.

My mother, family, and friends donate funds to the Transportation Program regularly. Also, interested foundations have given grants to the Georgia ALS Association to maintain the program. A portion of the royalties I receive from the sale of my books will also be donated to the Paul B. Williams ALS Transportation Program.

Travis Williams
February 2022

Acknowledgments

I thank God every day for my sweet mama, Linda Williams, a retired language arts teacher, who encouraged me to write this story, gave feedback on ideas, gave me impromptu grammar lessons, read, edited, proofread, and generally made it possible for me to create this book.

Paul B. Williams, my father, passed away with ALS before I started writing. One of the characters Uly meets is taken from a story my dad used to love to tell. He would have been cringing and laughing at Uly's predicaments. Please read more about my dad in the Afterword.

Lisa-Marie Haygood, Patti Sisk, Janet DeStazio, Jeffrey Taylor, and Justin Darby are friends and family who volunteered to read an early draft of the manuscript. Thank you for your insights and feedback.

Colleen McCubbin, my friend for over two decades, is a writer, publisher, and founder of Siretona Creative. She sent me a message one day asking what I had been up to lately.

I had been writing.

Almost a year later, I joined Siretona Creative's program for independent authors. We work together to share ideas, give tech support to each other, offer advice, proofread books, critique covers, attend one another's book launches, and generally support and cheer one another along. Colleen has created a great platform on which authors can thrive.

Nicola MacCameron, my fellow author and friend through Siretona Creative, read multiple early drafts of this book. She challenged me to expand the manuscript considerably and shared many ideas about how to improve it.

Charity Mongrain, Lisa LeBlanc, Marcia Laycock, Connie Inglis, and Robert Stermscheg are writers at Siretona Creative who have been gracious and encouraging readers of early drafts.

Louis at LouieBuilt Automotive explained what Uly needed to do to fix the church van. If I got that wrong, it's not his fault.

Harris Kuntry Meats—unlike the fictional businesses in the narrative—is a real store outside Hawkinsville that has great steaks and barbecue. I am delighted to mention them.

The owner of the real Victorian mansion that serves as inspiration for The MacAllister Victorian, was a gracious host. A mutual friend introduced me to him and helped him give me a tour of his wonderful house. As a result, Lucy's bed and breakfast is much more detailed and opulent.

Sandra Mersinger gave invaluable feedback and encouragement on the cover.

Claire Tucker edited the manuscript with a stunning eye for detail. She has an extraordinary capacity to make grammatically significant deep dives. This book is much better because of her recommendations.

Finally, I've learned I must rely on God. When I read my Bible, when I experience "peace that passes understanding," when I remember "the battle belongs to the Lord," God empowers and inspires me through his Holy Spirit in his son, Jesus Christ, to the glory of the Father. As a sweet centenarian lady living in a nursing home once said to me, "Trust in the Lord."

Amen.

About the Author

Travis Williams was born in Alabama and lives and writes from his home in Georgia at a desk in front of a window overlooking his backyard. He has designed logos, book covers, fonts, and he occasionally breaks out some paints. He writes fiction—Southern, science and historical—with Christian themes. He's online at BooksByTravis.com. *Uly Quits His Job* is his first novel.

Colophon

Uly Quits His Job was written on an iPad using Scrivener and Ulysses writing apps. The cover and map designs were completed using Affinity Photo and Affinity Designer. The body text is typeset in More Pro Book by Łukasz Dziedzic, of Warsaw Poland, and the map typeface is CA Postal by German designer Stefan Claudius. Hannah Cole at Bankert Marketing, Dauphin, Manitoba, Canada, designed the book layout using Adobe InDesign. Printed on 38# groundwood eggshell paper by The Ingram Book Company.